GHOSTS OF THE PAST

GRAND HUMAN EMPIRE BOOK 3

JOHN WILKER

EDITED BY
CHRISTINA SHORT

Rogue Publishing

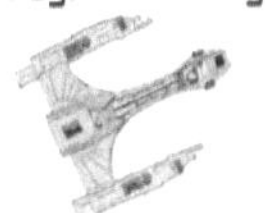

For my Wife, Nicole

CONTENTS

PART ONE

CHAPTER 1

Jax was standing in a windowless room full of uncomfortable-looking people sitting in equally uncomfortable-looking chairs. How, in the age of artificial gravity and wormhole-based travel, chairs could be uncomfortable, he wasn't sure.

His grounding at the hands and direct order of his adopted aunt, Governor Neeti Singh, was almost over. Being unable to fly for so long had been eating at him.

Next to him on the wall, a control panel lit up. He glanced down at it, then looked at the sea of expectant faces. "Turton, Richard." His gaze wandered until a hand raised above the crowd.

A thin man stood. "That's me." He had a faintly British accent. He kept his salt and pepper hair close cropped. He was wearing what was likely his best suit, tailored to his lanky frame. Everyone in the room was equally well dressed.

Jax nodded to the door next to him. "Through there." The other man nodded and entered, the door sliding closed behind him. Jax's gPhone beeped, and he pulled it from his pocket. A message from Skip, the Sapient Intelligence that managed his ship, the *Osprey*. His currently locked down ship. *I AM*

BORED is all the message said. Jax huffed and replied, *Less than a week.* He put his gPhone back in the pocket of his own suit slacks. His client insisted he wear a suit when on duty. It itched and was tight in all the wrong places. *YOU ARE NOT THE ONE BOLTED TO THE DECK*, the ship replied.

The door that led to the hallway beyond the waiting room slid open, and Rudy rolled in. The navigation droid had a steaming cup in one hand, the other folded against the cylindrical torso. He offered Jax the cup. "Here."

"Thanks." He took the cup, inhaling the aromatic steam. The interior door slid open, and the tall British guy from before rushed out. He hurried through the waiting room, a single sob escaping his lips before he was out the hatch and into the hallway beyond and gone.

"That might be a record," Jax said as the outer door slid closed.

Rudy's optic sensor followed the man, then turned to Jax. "She's still making them cry?"

Jax nodded. "Yeah. The one before him was downright wrecked. I asked station security to do a wellness check in a little bit." He took a sip of the drink Rudy brought him. Lab grown coffee. Not even remotely as good as the genuine stuff, but affordable. Naomi took what she brought home from New Terra with her when she shipped out with the Delphinos, forcing him back to the lab grown stuff. He might be on better terms with the brothers who made his childhood a living hell, but the thought of them enjoying delicious honest-to-God coffee from a plant that grew in dirt, irritated him.

He shook the thought away and looked at the still open interior door. "Part of me wants to be a fly on the wall in there. The other is really glad I'm not."

The door slid closed, and the panel next to him beeped. Jax sighed. "Riley? Sarah Riley?"

A woman in a charcoal-colored pencil skirt raised her hand. "That's me." She tied her pale hair into a ponytail that reached the small of her back. She stood, and he motioned to the door next to him.

Rudy bobbed on his smart material ball. "Heard from Naomi?"

Jax took another sip. "Did you tell them extra sugar?"

The droid made a whirring noise. "You're too fat. You need less sugar." Changing the material of his rollerball, making it adhesive, Rudy tilted at a thirty-degree angle from the deck, narrowly avoiding Jax's swipe. Straightening up, he said, "Don't change the subject."

Jax held up a finger and shushed the droid. "I am within the acceptable body mass range for my age group. But, no. She checked in when they reached Bethesda, but I haven't heard from her since. They should be on their way home by now. I think."

"Everyone ready?" Marshall asked from the pilot's station of the *Buttercup*, the Delphino brothers' freighter. The hold was empty, their client having finished unloading the ship an hour before.

The ship was sitting on its landing pad in the Johnston Spaceport. Rivulets of rain were winding their way down the transparent viewscreen that wrapped the forward third of the bridge.

From the lounge, a short flight of stairs from the flight deck, Steve and Naomi shouted, "All set." They were enjoying a beer at the small dining table bolted to the deck.

Naomi looked across the table to Steve. "Thanks again."

The younger Delphino shrugged. "We needed someone, and you were available." He smiled. "Plus, I couldn't pass up the opportunity to mess with Jax. His being grounded is just too hilarious."

Naomi shook her head. "Yeah, the idea of being cooped up on Kelso while he went out of his mind wasn't that appealing." She held her bottle up in a toast. "This has been fun." He clinked his bottle against hers.

The ship rumbled as its thrusters powered up. The deck tilted as the *Buttercup* rose off the permacrete of Johnston Spaceport.

The rain hadn't let up the entire time the *Buttercup* had been on Bethesda Three. The Delphinos had been hired to deliver four tons of weather-hardy grain to the local coop on Bethesda Three—a job the *Osprey* could never take but that left the *Buttercup* with room to spare for a side job Marshall had arranged.

Thirty minutes later, Marshall joined them in the lounge, the rumble of the freighter's engines settling into a steady thrum as she pushed clear of the planet's gravity. "We'll be clear for wormhole in thirty or so minutes." He dropped into a ratty chair that seemed to be more duct tape than upholstery. He looked around. "You guys look at the take yet?"

Steve smiled. "We waited for you." He rose and walked a beer over to his brother.

The three chatted over their beers until the ceiling speaker beeped twice, alerting Marshall that the *Buttercup* had reached the minimum safe distance to open a wormhole. Any closer to a planetary mass, and things tended to go poorly—for the ship and the planet.

Marshall stood and walked back to the small bridge. A few minutes later, he came back. He pointed to the corridor that ran along the spine of the large vessel. The staircase at the end went to the hold and engineering. "Ready?"

Naomi smiled, rising from her chair. "Is this the kind of thing you two get up to a lot?"

Steve stood, and the three headed down the corridor. He looked over his shoulder. "It pays better than hauling seeds."

Marshall sniggered. "He's not wrong."

The *Buttercup* was five times the size of the *Osprey*. The corridor that ran the length of the ship had hatches every four meters: crew quarters, a med bay that was in worse shape than the *Osprey*'s, and a few supply rooms. The staircase at the end of the corridor dropped to engineering, then continued on to the large hold that made up the bulk of the ship. In the corner, near the large forward cargo doors, were two crates, each taller than Naomi.

Both cases had a keypad on one side. Marshall tapped a sequence into the pad, and with a hiss, the lid rose.

Naomi rose up on her toes to peer inside the case. She couldn't see much but could smell it. "Is that...?"

"Tapioca?" Steve said.

"Yup." Marshall beamed. "Stuff is more valuable than gold."

Naomi turned, her face scrunched. "To who?"

"Whom," Steve corrected. Naomi didn't move, but her eyes twitched to the side to glare at the younger man, who held both hands up defensively.

Marshall closed the lid. "The Brazilian colonies love the stuff." He tapped the key to lock the case. "We can get three times what we paid, within a few hours of landing."

Naomi shrugged. "Well, it's better than guns."

Marshall frowned. "You thought we ran guns?"

Naomi shrugged again. Before she could reply, the ship shook, then canted sideways hard enough that the grav-generator couldn't keep up, sending the three of them skidding across the cargo hold deck. If the two crates of tapioca hadn't been strapped down, they would have crushed Naomi against the bulkhead.

Jax was beginning to think Sarah Riley might be the one. She had been in the room with his client for longer than any other applicant so far. Then the door slid open and the blonde woman walked out, eyes red from crying. She made her way to the outer door.

A woman in her mid-fifties stepped into the open doorway. She looked around the room, then to Jax, next to the door frame. "Losers, all of them." The applicants nearest to them cast uneasy glances at each other, then at Jax, then at his client: Fatima Agarwal.

Jax smiled. "Ms. Agarwal, you have to hire one."

She clucked, "Don't remind me."

The Agarwal family, while not a founding family, had quickly become one of the more prominent families on Kelso station. Her grandmother's mastery of shipping and logistics, paired with her grandfather's culinary expertise, led to a restaurant chain with four locations on Kelso and three more on other stations, plus a few dozen franchises on various planets.

"Maybe if you were nicer," Rudy offered, then rolled back a

foot as the bespoke suit-wearing woman took a menacing step towards him. She had her dark hair pulled into a tight bun, two lethal-looking needles holding it together forming an X. She turned to Jax. "Send in the next one." She didn't wait for him to reply, turning back into the inner office beyond.

Jax once again thought back on the choices that had resulted in him having to take this job. He'd tried more than once in the last three weeks to appeal to his aunt to lift her grounding early. Each time, she fed him and sent him on his way without lifting her ruling. He even tried bribing Lewis, one of the Kelso station customs agents, to no avail. The grav-locks that Governor Singh ordered turned on were keeping the *Osprey* firmly locked down in the Caruso family mechanical bay for four more days. Against the advice of Rudy, he had even tried getting to them from under the deck plating, only to receive a shock that left his toes numb for two days.

He summoned the next applicant, a woman in a teal pants suit with multi-colored scarf. As she passed him, she winked and said, "Wish me luck."

Jax watched the door slide closed and made a note of her name.

Rudy's squat head spun a full three hundred and sixty degrees. "Okay, I'm leaving now. Baxter asked me to pick up an actuator assembly for his railguns."

"How much did that cost?" Jax asked.

The droid was halfway across the small waiting room. He waved a hand. "You don't want to know. I had to get two because they come in pairs and haven't been made in about fifteen years."

Jax sighed.

Rudy rolled to the exit, and as the droid rolled out into the hallway, a middle-aged man in a nice, but not tailored, suit walked in. Jax shook his head. "No chance," he mumbled, watching the new arrival find a seat and attempt small talk with the woman next to him.

CHAPTER 2

After a few minutes, the new arrival stood and moved toward the center of the waiting room. "Everyone down!" he shouted, pulling a pulse pistol out from the waistband of his slacks. Job applicants screamed and scrambled to the floor, overturning chairs and other applicants in the process.

"Damnit," Jax hissed. He slipped a hand into his pocket, tapping the screen of his gPhone a few times. He slowly kneeled down, along with the rest of the applicants. After composing his best friendly smile, he said, "Hey, buddy. I remember you. Marvin, right?"

The man frowned. "My name is Kevin!" he screamed. Jax opened his mouth. "Shut up!" the man screamed, far louder than necessary in the small space. He stepped further into the space, stepping around limbs and sobbing bodies. He kicked a woman who was sobbing too loudly, eliciting a scream. He turned his focus back to Jax. "She in there?"

"Who?" Jax asked, still on his knees. "You know, weapons need to be registered on Kelso."

The man squinted. "What?" He shook his head. "Don't

fuck with me, man!" He waved the pistol from Jax to the door to the inner office. "Is that bitch Agarwal in there?"

The door behind Jax slid open, and the pants suited woman stepped out. "Thank you so much, ma'am. I'm excited to get —" She saw Jax on his knees and the man with the gun, and screamed as she stumbled backward.

Jax took his chance. The sudden arrival of Pants Suit Woman and her subsequent scream confused the gunman. Jax lunged, tackling the man, driving his shoulder into the man's midsection. This caused more screams from the terrified applicants. Several tried to scramble out of the tussling pair's path. Miss Pants Suit scrambled back into the interior office. Jax heard Ms. Agarwal shout an obscenity or two before the door slid closed.

From the door to the outer corridor, Rudy said, "Attention, please. Everyone come this way." His voice was louder than normal and full of authority. When no one moved, he raised his voice a few more decibels. "I said move, now!"

Jax and gunman were rolling around, Jax's hand clamped on the man's wrist, keeping the pistol aimed away from him. The angry ex-applicant squeezed off a few shots, scorching the wall. The few remaining applicants in the room screamed and scrambled through the hatch, shoving Rudy aside.

Jax looked up to shout orders at Rudy, but a flailing fist clipped him in the jaw, sending him lurching off of his opponent.

The gunman jumped up and rushed the interior door, slamming his free hand against the access panel. The panel answered his angry attacks with subtle beeps and a blinking red indicator.

Before Jax could regain his feet, Rudy rolled in, knives polished to an immaculate gleam in each hand. As he rolled, his torso spun, turning him into a rust-colored murder tornado.

"What the hell?" the gunman shouted. He fired twice, Rudy dodging expertly. A knife sliced across the back of the man's hand, his gun clattering to the deck. He looked down at Rudy, dodging another spinning knife attack. He moved to reach for the gun, only to be tackled by Jax.

The outer door opened, and two Kelso station security officers rushed in. Rudy stopped spinning, stashing his knives in their compartment on his cylindrical torso in a fluid motion.

The female security officer kicked the gun away while her partner lifted the gunman out from under Jax.

Jax nodded. "Thanks."

The female officer smiled. "Thank your little friend. He called us." She tilted her head toward Rudy. "I saw the knives, by the way."

Rudy rolled in a circle. "Beep, boop." He shrugged.

The gunman struggled. "She has to pay. She can't treat people this way."

The male security officer looked around. "Uh, who?"

Jax snapped his fingers. "Oh, shit." He tapped in a sequence on the access panel. The red light blinked and went out. The door slid open.

Fatima Agarwal said from inside, "It's safe?" Before anyone could answer, Pants Suit Woman stumbled out into the waiting room. She scowled, looking back.

"It's clear, ma'am," Jax said.

The restauranteur leaned out. She saw the gunman, who saw her and renewed his struggling against the security officers. The female officer shook the man. "Stop that!" She turned to Jax, then Agarwal. "I'll need a statement."

Jax nodded. "I'll stop by the station in a bit." The woman nodded and gestured for her partner to head out.

Jax looked at his client, then the younger woman in the pants suit. "So?"

The older woman frowned. "Yes, she got the job."

Jax smiled at the new executive assistant to Fatima Agarwal. "Congrats, and good luck."

He turned to leave and felt his gPhone vibrate. Looking at the screen as he exited the waiting room, he saw a contact card pop up.

Before the door slid closed, he heard Agarwal say, "First order of business. Call the remaining applicants and tell them they're out of luck."

"I told you we should have waited on that firmware update," Steve groaned. He, Marshall, and Naomi had managed to get to the *Buttercup*'s cramped computer center. The ship was on a ballistic course out of the system. They had passed their intended wormhole point a few minutes ago. Naomi hoped that space control was watching and, with any luck, had sent help.

Marshall aimed the flashlight at his brother's face. "Shut up." He turned the beam back to the processing core.

"Space control should be sending help," Naomi offered.

Marshall made a face, his ears reddening. "Well. Probably not."

"What?" Steve and Naomi demanded in unison.

The bigger Delphino rubbed the back of his neck. "I turn off our transponder once we leave orbit."

"Why?" Naomi planted her hands on her hips. "We didn't do anything illegal."

Marshall shrugged. "Habit."

His brother sighed. "So, we're ballistic and no one knows." He turned to Naomi, behind his brother's back, eyebrows arched. In the dim light, he could see her face and her lack of understanding of what he was implying. He wiggled his eyebrows, then raised a hand and wiggled his fingers.

She rolled her eyes and motioned for him to stop. After taking a breath, she said, "We should check the reactor." She paused, trying to think of a reason.

Steve got there first. "She's right, the reactor might be in a loop."

"A loop?" Marshall repeated, once again blinding his brother with the flashlight.

Steve put a hand in front of his face and said, "Yeah, let's check that." He looked past Marshall to Naomi. "Stay here and see if anything changes."

She nodded, rolling her eyes. "Sure thing."

Once the two Delphinos had left the computer room and Naomi couldn't hear their bickering, she turned to the computer interface mounted to the processing core. As far as she could tell, the core was online, just not functioning. Naomi rested her hands on the sides of the terminal. Her bio-circuits illuminated, pulsing blue as she reached out to the comatose core.

With her eyes closed, Naomi could sense more than see the computer core and its programming. The core was online, receiving power. She couldn't sense any faults or alerts. Then she found it, the firmware update Steve had mentioned. It was meant to improve the processing core's handling of input/output, making most functions markedly faster. Except it wasn't complete. Code was there but unexecuted. The old code was removed from the processing core's runtime. Something had happened that caused the update to derail.

Naomi's bio-circuit tattoos pulsed as she shuffled code, finding the original firmware update routine, executing it.

The lights in the computer center blinked to life. Over the ship wide intercom, Marshall said, "Hey, Naomi, the power is back. What did you do?"

She frowned, her tattoos dimming until they weren't distinguishable from her skin. She shook her head and said, "I'm good with computers." She heard Steve chuckle in the background.

From the overhead speaker, Marshall said, "I'll get us back on course."

Back in the small crew lounge, Naomi was giving Steve a hard time. "Not okay. If I wanted everyone to know about my abilities, I'd add it to my station bio."

Steve held up both hands, palms out. "Sorry. I wasn't thinking." He took a sip of his drink. "Well, I was thinking—about not dying in the deep dark recesses of space, my body turning into a desiccated husk when the environmental systems give out."

She waved his reply away. "Just be careful. Your brother is really low on the list of people I want knowing about..." She held up her free hand, bio-circuits glowing. "This."

Steve dipped his head. "Cool, and sorry. Good work, though. What was it?"

Naomi made a show of sipping her beer, then said, "Firmware update. I'm guessing Marshall removed the drive before the process was complete."

Steve shook his head. "Moron."

Jax walked out of the main security center and looked around the open space before him. The Kelso station security office was off of one of the promenade decks, offering a wide view and open space rather than the bare metal, three-meter-wide corridors that made up most of the station access ways.

Rudy, waiting outside the station, rolled over. "All done?"

Jax nodded. "Yeah." He looked at his gPhone. "I was thinking I'd head to the Ang—"

"Your aunt wants to see you," the meter-tall nav droid interrupted.

Jax closed his mouth. "Uh, okay." He looked at Rudy. "Why didn't she call me?"

The droid made his exasperated noise as his head rotated in a full three hundred and sixty degrees. "Faraday cage." He pointed to the hatch behind Jax.

Jax turned. "Oh, yeah." He looked across the open area littered with vendor stalls and grassy areas for station citizens to enjoy. "Coming?"

The droid turned and rolled away, saying, "Nope."

"Dick," Jax hissed as he headed across the space toward the

central column that contained the lifts and other equipment that ran the length of the station. As he entered the lift car, his gPhone beeped. He pressed the icon for the government section of the station, then looked at the screen. Ms. Agarwal had paid his invoice. He smiled.

The government offices of Kelso station were near the top of the cigar-shaped central structure. The lift car emptied into a wide waiting area. Offices lined the outer perimeter: the customs office, taxes and excise, permitting, and things Jax didn't understand. At opposite ends of the wide circular space sat the governor's and lieutenant governor's offices.

Jax never understood why they were so far apart. His aunt had tried explaining the reasoning, but he always tuned the story out a minute or two in.

The double doors to the governor's outer office slid apart. "Hey, Jeffry," Jax said before the younger man even looked up from his work.

The station governor's administrative assistant didn't even look up. "She's expecting you." He pointed to the double doors next to his work station.

Jax approached the ornate doors, which slid apart as he neared. From inside he heard, "Come in, Jackson."

"Hi, Auntie!" Jax said, feigning joviality. He moved to the seat opposite her. "You wanted to see me?"

Governor Neeti Singh looked up from the tablet she was working on. "Fati said you did a good job for her."

Jax shook his head. "The network never misses a beat, does it? I'm glad she's happy with the service rendered."

The governor smiled. "I'm proud of you."

Jax did a double take. "For what?"

"Well, you did protect her."

Jax laughed. "From a disgruntled dude that she probably made cry the day prior? Wasn't a tough job."

The elderly governor smiled, her eyes bright as ever. "Either way, you took a legit job and finished it. I've already instructed customs to remove the grav-lock on the *Osprey*."

Jax leaped out of his seat. "Yes!" He pumped a fist in the air.

His adopted aunt clucked, "Was it really so bad? You only had three more days."

Jax sat back down, his grin still ear to ear. "Three long days, to go with the twenty-seven that came before them. I love you, Auntie, but this has been hell."

"Don't be so melodramatic."

"I'm not meant to be on the ground this long." Jax leaned forward.

"You're on a space station, Jackson." She clucked again and stood. The armoire next to her desk was always kept closed. She opened it, revealing a dizzying array of bottles, their contents a rainbow of liquors. She retrieved a bottle and poured its contents into two tumblers. Offering one to Jax, she said, "Promise me you won't do anything stupid now that you're free." She held her tumbler up in a toast.

Jax raised his own glass. "No promises." He grinned before downing the amber liquid.

CHAPTER 3

Wormhole travel had revolutionized space travel for humanity, allowing people to expand to distant star systems as rapidly as they could. It wasn't a perfect system, however. Communication within a wormhole was impossible, at least as far as human science had determined. Ships were effectively blind to the outside galaxy while traveling through wormholes.

The *Buttercup* had dropped out of her wormhole to re-orient for the last leg of the return trip back to Kelso station. Wormholes were also straight lines. Ships had to return to normal space to make course adjustments, collect messages from the nearest galactic Internex node, and check for navigation hazards.

Naomi's gPhone beeped. She was sitting in her berth watching one of the Delphino brothers' stored entertainment vids. Not a very good one. She looked at the screen. A message from Jax: *FREEDOM. PARTY AT THE SPACER.*

She tapped a reply and un-paused the video. Her gPhone beeped again. *FINE. BRING THE DUMMIES.* She smiled.

The wall display flashed a red outline around the program

Naomi was watching, and a countdown timer appeared in the top left corner. One minute until wormhole entry.

Naomi rapped her knuckles on the bridge hatch. "So, Jax is free."

Marshall groaned. "That's good, right? He won't be all moody now."

Steve clucked. "I doubt it. Isn't this a few days early?"

Naomi dropped into the small jump seat against the rear bulkhead. Somehow, despite being nearly five times the size of the *Osprey*, the bridge of the *Buttercup* was maybe half the size of the smaller ship's bridge, which wasn't what one would call spacious.

She said, "He didn't elaborate. But he's throwing a get together at the Angry Spacer tomorrow night, station time."

Steve checked the console before him. "We should arrive at Kelso tomorrow midday, so..."

"Drinks on Jackie!" Marshall whooped.

Naomi rolled her eyes. "Dinner? My treat, or well, my labor. I'm cooking."

Marshall turned. "How's your linguine alle vongole?"

"I don't know what that is."

"Tagliatelle alla boscaiola?"

"Are you just making up words?"

Marshall sighed. "What are you going to make?"

Naomi winked. "Tacos."

Marshall grumbled about originality, and something about quality, under his breath as he put his console into standby while the ship's RI, or Rudimentary Intelligence, the simpler cousin to Skip, took over the flying. RIs, while not sapient, were exceptional at the tasks they were designed for. The one on the *Buttercup* had one job: keep the ship from hitting the side of the wormhole. It didn't even have a name. The two Delphino brothers just called it "ship."

While Naomi worked in the kitchenette, the two Delphinos lounged on the couch talking about something, but she couldn't hear. Steve craned his neck. "You know, I kinda expected, I dunno, an Asian dish."

Naomi stopped what she was doing. "Why? Because I'm Asian?" She made air quotes over the last word. "Because all I know how to make are noodles? Raw fish?"

Marshall's eyebrows shot up as far as they physically could. He looked at his brother, his face making it clear he was not about to jump in and help.

Steve stammered, "Well, no. I mean..."

Naomi affected a mocking nasally tone. "I make you sushi, wontons, like fried rice?"

Marshall bit his lip to keep his face under control. Steve's face turned a deep crimson.

Naomi stared at Steve until she couldn't keep her face straight. "God!" She doubled over. "You're such an easy mark." She straightened, turning back to the cooktop. "I can do some mean makizushi, but you goombas are a bit lacking on ingredients that aren't starches."

Marshall finally exhaled. "Oh, man. I really wish I'd recorded that. It was priceless."

Steve slugged his older brother in the shoulder. "Shut up."

The bigger Delphino returned the gesture, almost knocking his brother off the sofa.

Lucas smiled when Jax walked in. "If it's not the birthday boy!"

Jax frowned. "It's not..."

The cybernetically enhanced bartender waved the comment away. "'Recently ungrounded grown ass man' doesn't have the same ring to it." He set about pouring Jax a drink.

Jax shrugged as he took a seat at the bar. "Fair enough." He accepted the drink.

Lucas pointed toward the back. "I set up your little party, back there." The bartender had festooned the long table in the back with banners, balloons, and streamers, all proclaiming *Happy Birthday!*

Jax looked, nodded, and turned back to Lucas. "Really?"

"Like I said. Spacer Wares doesn't have a section for 'grown ass man grounded by his aunt for being bad.' Go figure." He shrugged.

Jax flipped him off while raising his glass.

The other man inclined his head. "Don't you think this is a bit, you know, much? I mean, it was only a month."

"A month that felt like ten years," Jax replied.

Lewis, the customs agent, walked in. "Oh hi, Jax!" He

waved from the entry.

As the portly little customs man walked over, Lucas said, "Lewis?"

Jax shrugged. "I'm not exactly rolling deep in the friends department." As if to punctuate that statement, the short older woman that hustled dart tournaments walked in. "Laz!" Jax shouted, raising his glass. Lucas rolled his eyes and set about preparing a drink.

Lewis took a seat next to Jax, clapping a hand on his shoulder as he ordered tonic water.

"Jackson, you space scoundrel. You're back sailing among the stars?" Laz winked at Lucas, who set about pouring her drink from the shaker he had just used to make it.

Jax smiled. "Good to see ya, Laz. No dart tourneys lately?"

The tiny old woman grunted. "Station security has been paying a bit too much attention of late. Something about someone complaining that I hustled them." She scowled.

Jax looked at the ceiling, then stood, motioning her and Lewis to join him at the birthday table.

Lewis, following behind, said, "It's your birthday, too? I thought that was in February."

Laz looked up at him, then turned to Jax. "Invite him to my next tournament."

From the entry, someone—not just someone, but Marshall Delphino—shouted, "Jackie!"

Jax's shoulders bunched. He turned to see the two Delphinos flanking Naomi, his business partner. The trio waved to Lucas as they made their way toward the back of the bar.

Naomi reached the back of the Spacer. She looked around at the motley assortment of "friends" and the decorations hanging from the bulkhead and attached to the table. "Happy birthday?" Jax groaned, "Don't ask." He handed her his glass and waved to Lucas to get another beer.

Steve walked up, offering his fist for Jax to knock his own against. "Happy birthday!" he said, mock excitement bubbling up into his wide grin.

Jax made a rude gesture.

Lucas arrived with Jax's drink, a New Terra Lager. He took the Delphinos' orders and walked back to the bar.

Jax looked at his partner and sorta friends. "How'd your run to Bethesda go?"

Naomi opened her mouth, but Marshall cut her off. "Great. Happy client. Invoice paid."

Naomi hitched a thumb toward the larger Delphino. "Did you know they...well, it's not really smuggling, I guess...deal in tapioca?"

Marshall made a face.

Jax looked at her, then the two brothers. "Tapioca?"

"Pays the bills," Marshall offered. He turned to Naomi. "Thought we weren't talking about it."

Naomi shrugged. "It's not as interesting a secret as you think."

"Pays the bills and then some," Steve added. "Plus, it's not illegal and won't get us grounded." He smirked.

Jax pulled a face, then turned as Jeffry, his aunt's administrative assistant, walked in. The younger man took three steps into the Spacer and looked around, smoothed his shirt twice and marched toward the *Happy Birthday* banners. When he reached Jax and the others, he said, "This place is...interesting." He looked around, then turned to the table, picking at something on the surface. "Does station health services know it's here?"

Jax poked the other man in the chest, hard. "You'll say nothing about this place." He looked past Jeffry to the bar and made a motion. Lucas nodded.

Two hours and dozens of drinks later, the party had turned to Jax, Naomi, and the Delphinos drinking and popping balloons. Lewis had been the first to depart; Jax had put money on it being Jeffry. He was the second, though. Laz and a few other folks from the station hung on for a while before fading away, congratulating Jax on his return to freedom as they departed.

Jax said, "Let's take this elsewhere."

Steve raised an eyebrow.

Naomi looked around and said, "Uh, no, bro cloud." She looked at each man in turn. "No."

Jax said, "I meant, off station." He looked at Naomi, then Steven, shaking his head. "Thirsty." He stood up. "Del Rio is only two hours from here." He motioned for them to follow. "Come on. I know this outstanding diner on Del Rio Two, in Commerce Dome 14, or maybe it's 15? Either way, it's good." He marched off, not waiting for any of them to follow.

Naomi turned to the two Delphinos and shrugged. She finished her drink and stood up. "Come on, it'll be fun."

Steve looked at his brother and said, "We've got nothing else to do." The bigger Delphino downed the remains of his drink and stood.

—

"Kelso space control, *Osprey* departing," Jax said, a grin splitting his face. Beyond the transparent viewport of the bridge, the orange strobes were swirling. The massive space doors of the Caruso family mechanical bay were wide open. The only thing keeping the atmosphere in was the static atmosphere barrier, shimmering faintly here and there as dust particles struck it.

From the speaker on his console came the reply, "Copy that, *Osprey*. Try not to get into any more trouble." Before Jax could reply, the light showing that the comm line was active went out.

"Everyone's got jokes," Jax said, pushing the power lever for the lift engines forward, increasing their thrust.

From the same speaker, Skip said, "I can't tell you how happy I am to be getting out of this hangar."

Jax nodded as he throttled up the engines to guide the ship away from Kelso station. The station's traffic control system automatically fed data to the ship's navigation computer.

For the *Osprey*, that was Rudy. The squat nav droid processed the incoming data stream and pushed the important bits to one of the displays in front of Jax. Guide lines appeared to help the *Osprey* out of local space and away from potential collisions. He said, "Course plotted. Wormhole distance in five minutes."

"Copy that. Wanna go play bartender?"

"No."

Jax turned and glared at his mechanical friend. "I'm sorry, that sounded like a request." He made a shooing motion.

Once Rudy was gone, Jax sat in silence for a few minutes, watching the controls as the distance to wormhole entry counted down and the distance from Kelso station counted up. Outside the viewport, the stars of deep space shone, bright pinpricks of light.

"Jackson," the ceiling said.

"Yeah, Skip."

"Don't do anything stupid again, that gets you...me... grounded. That was the longest month of my life."

Jax smirked. "It was rough for me, too."

A noise like a scoff or grunt came out of the speaker. "I process time thousands of times faster than you. While not exact, the lack of activity or even company was comparable to about four hundred human years. Roughly." Jax made a choked sound. Skip said, "Exactly."

The countdown to safe wormhole distance hit zero. Jax powered up the wormhole generator, watching the diagnostics run. When the board was green, he pressed the button activating the device. Tremendous amounts of exotic energy poured out of the *Osprey*, forcing a rip in space-time to appear directly ahead.

Once the ship was safely traveling many times the speed of light through the condensed space-time of the wormhole, Jax stood. He looked at the ceiling. "I'll do my best, buddy." He took the stairs down to the common deck.

The small flight deck was empty. Skip said to no one, "That does not reassure me."

CHAPTER 4

Del Rio Two wasn't one of those picturesque colonies that had blue skies with friendly, puffy clouds, tree-lined parks, and colonists walking about carefree. It was a brownish gray color, dotted with domes. The thin atmosphere had no clouds.

Anyone walking around outside the colony domes would die a horrible asphyxiating death as their skin melted off their bodies.

The domes that dotted the surface of Del Rio Two were a mix of transparent and the uniform grey of permacrete. The *Osprey* landed in Public Docking Dome 18. One of the larger domes, the interior had two interior rings, one third and two-thirds up the side of the dome. Each was smaller than the one below, designed for smaller vessels.

The *Osprey* wasn't large enough to warrant space on the floor of the dome, so space control assigned her a spot on the middle ring. As steam vented from the engine cowlings, the boarding ramp dropped to the reinforced permacrete shelf.

The two-hour trip from Kelso to the Del Rio system had been spent nearly emptying Jax's shipboard liquor cabinet. Marshall was the first down the boarding ramp. He caught his toe on something and went head over heels to end up sprawled across the platform, swearing up a storm as he came to a stop.

Jax and Naomi followed, the former clucking, "Don't fall off the platform, Marshmallow. You know they charge the ship for the cleanup." He offered a hand to the larger man, hauling him up.

Steve walked down the ramp. He looked up from his gPhone. "Lift, that way." He pointed along the gently curving wall of the dome. A few landing pads to the right of theirs, a reinforced lift cage ran up to the next landing ring and down to the ground below.

A network of transit tunnels with mag-lev trains running between them connected the domes of Del Rio Two. The larger domes had more than one line coming and going.

The transit station in Commerce Dome 14 was not one of the nicer ones. Seeing that it wasn't in a particularly upscale dome, that made sense.

The transit car doors slid apart, allowing the group to stumble out. "Oh, my God," Naomi wheezed. She pinched her nose. "Is this dome open to atmosphere?"

Jax laughed. "No, that's the pet food plant." He took a deep breath. "They're doing puppy chow this week."

"Gross," Marshall said.

Steve took a deep breath. "Don't they vent that out of the dome?"

Jax shrugged and pointed to a corridor that led further into the dome.

After ten minutes of walking through trash strewn corridors and dodging some sort of winged vermin none of them were familiar with, Naomi looked at the boarded-up building. "So, best diner on Del Rio Two?"

Jax looked at his friends. "I mean, that title was subjective." He held his hands out, palms up.

Steve looked around. "So...."

Naomi offered, "Maybe it was Commerce Dome 15?"

Marshall pointed up the street. It was near local midnight, and not much was open. "I could go for a bloomin' onion."

Everyone turned. Steve said, "That's a TGI Friday's. They don't do the bloomin' onion."

"Who does?"

As they made their way up the block, Naomi said, "Are you sure?"

Steve nodded.

"I think the bloomin' onion is Outback Steakhouse. They went under a dozen or more years back. At least out here," Steve answered.

"No, I think it was Chili's," Naomi replied.

Steve shook his head. "No, theirs was the awesome blossom." He sighed. "I miss Chili's. I think they got bought by one of the tech firms, then closed down."

Despite the hour, the TGI Friday's was busy. They got a booth in the bar section and promptly ordered drinks and mozzarella sticks.

When the server walked away, Jax said, "We had these on Nuevo Santiago. They're good."

The drinks arrived, and Jax held his up. "To me."

"Gauche," Naomi said, raising her glass.

Jax smiled. "Whatever. I've been grounded for a month working for the sausage queen of Kelso station, whom I think might be a legit sociopath. I deserve this." He pushed his drink higher. "Cheers, motherfuckers."

Everyone raised their glasses, shaking their heads.

Consciousness came slowly. Jax's heavy eyelids fluttered, letting in the dim light. "Ugh." He moved a hand to rub his face before opening his eyes. His face felt like sandpaper, stubble lining his cheeks and chin. He wasn't sure, but his tongue might have had stubble on it also. Sitting up, he looked around. He was in possibly the dingiest room he could remember ever being in. A single light fixture in the ceiling glowed faintly.

Naomi was snoring in the bed next to him. He couldn't remember leaving the TGI Friday's, let alone finding a motel, of some sort, to check into. He took stock: he was still dressed, and his boots were off. He looked to Naomi's bed. She was still dressed, her boots on the floor next to the bed.

A buzzing in his pocket startled him. He glanced at Naomi, still snoring. He looked at the device. A message from Steve: YOU UP? He tapped a reply and slid out of bed as slowly as possible. As he was lacing up his boots, Steve replied, NOT EVEN CLOSE TO WHAT I WAS THINKING. BREAKFAST?

Jax rubbed his temples with both hands, then tapped out his

reply. He stood, slipped into his boots, and headed for the door. Outside the door, he got a better picture of where they were. He was on the top floor of a two-story motel. There were a few hover cars parked in the lot below, and at the end of the street, a diner.

The door to the room next to his opened, and Steve leaned out. He winced at the light being generated by the illumination elements mounted along the support beams for the dome. The Del Rio Two atmosphere was far too thick for much sunlight to reach the surface. Jax pointed to the diner on the corner, eyebrow raised.

Steve shrugged. "Looks suitably shithole." He tilted his head. "Let's go."

"Where's Marshmallow?" Jax fell in next to his friend.

"Snoring loudly. Naked, somehow." The younger Delphino shuddered. "No idea when or why he ended up naked. Or how." He turned. "Naomi?"

"Also snoring, but fully clothed."

"Your loss." Jax nodded.

The diner, originally named Tom's, but maybe currently called just Diner, was as underwhelming as the two men expected. "Sit wherever," a heavyset woman in a stained apron said as she hustled past the two of them, a steaming coffee carafe in one hand, a dingy and dented tablet in the other. Jax pointed to a booth.

The waitress slowed as she passed. "Coffees?" They nodded. She did not slow down.

Steve watched the woman disappear around a corner, then turned to Jax. "So, feel good to be free?"

Jax smiled. The unfriendly server slid two thick ceramic mugs onto the table. The two men looked up. "Food," she said. It might not have been a question.

Jax said, "Pancakes, scrambled eggs, extra bacon." He

looked to Steve, who tilted his head, then said, "Same." The woman tapped on her tablet, then left.

Jax sipped his coffee, spat it back into the mug, and slid it to the far side of the table. He made a face, then looked at Steve. "So, how's What's His Face?"

"Walter? Oh, he's fine. Things kinda fizzled." Steve tried his own coffee. He made a pained face. "That is horrible." He slid his mug over next to Jax's.

Jax nodded. "Sorry, man. He seemed nice. Old, but nice."

Steve shrugged. "Still getting the hang of things. It's fine."

"Good outlook. Lotta men in the galaxy."

Steve held up a hand. "Woah, there, Slutty Spice."

Before Jax could reply, plates loaded with pancakes, eggs, and bacon slid onto the table. "Enjoy." She eyed the coffee mugs. "Refills?"

"No," Jax and Steve said in unison, placing their hands on top of the thick ceramic vessels.

From the booth next to them, behind Jax, a voice said, "So, look, I found something. Something huge. I've been sitting on this a while now and it's killin' me." The other occupant made a disbelieving noise. "Serious. I found them. The Nemesis Fleet."

Steve shoveled a fork full of eggs into his mouth. He chewed. "Okay, damn. These are pretty good."

"Shut up!" Jax hissed, leaning back. He made a motion to indicate he was listening to the conversation in the next booth.

Steve made a face. "What're you do—" Jax snapped vigorously, silencing him.

Steve made a face, then grabbed a piece of bacon off of Jax's plate.

From the other booth, a different voice said, "Are you daft? People have been looking for the Nemesis Fleet for, what? Two decades? You found it like I found that spot my wife says I never can hit."

Jax made a face. Steve looked at him again. "What?" He couldn't hear the conversation from his side of the table.

Jax scooted over and motioned Steve to join him on his side of the booth.

The first voice said, "Your pathetic sex life aside...I did. I found it. I was dodging an Imperial patrol a few months back and had to go extra ecliptic. It was a blind jump, we came out of the wormhole and nearly collided with a frigate."

Steve's eyes went wide.

The second voice, the one with the disappointed wife, said, "So, where is it?"

"No way. I saved the coordinates and stashed them somewhere safe. Then I wiped my nav system and everything. I even made sure the guys I was running that job with wouldn't be an issue, ever."

"What? Why?"

"Why? You idiot, it's a task force worth of antique ships. It's worth billions on the black market. I couldn't risk someone getting their hands on the coordinates before I was ready to move on it. What's that old saying? Three can keep a secret if two are dead. Well, it applies to five just the same. That's why I'm here talking to your dumb ass. I need your crew."

Toward the end of the Unification War, the Independent Systems Alliance fleet launched a task force of droid crewed warships to a secret waypoint until their human crews could rendezvous with them. That was the plan, at least.

Unfortunately for the Indies, the final battle of the war took place sooner than they had planned, and the human crews never arrived. Worse still, the officers that knew the location of the task force were killed, taking the coordinates of what they had hoped would be their overwhelming force to the grave.

The Nemesis Fleet, as it had been nicknamed, was lost. It became one of those legends that treasure hunters never tired of hunting for.

The two mystery booth neighbors continued talking over the logistics of salvaging the Nemesis Fleet while Jax and Steve listened intently, eating their breakfast as quietly as possible, waving the server away every time she came around.

From the other booth, the second man finally said, "Okay. I'll make some calls and we'll regroup. Where?"

The first guy answered. "I'm parked in Dome 7. Main level, Pad 17. The *Albright*."

"All right, see you later." The man stood and walked past Jax and Steve's booth. He glanced down at the two of them, sitting together on the same side of the booth. "Get a room homos," he growled, not slowing down.

The other man departed a few minutes later. Steve had moved back to his side of the booth by then. He and Jax watched the man leave.

Jax used his fork to shove cold eggs around his plate. He looked at Steve. "The Nemesis Fleet. You think?"

The younger Delphino shrugged. "Frumpy Smuggler Guy certainly seems to think so." He made to grab the last piece of bacon only to have his hand slapped. Withdrawing, bacon-less, he said, "How many ships were in that fleet? Can you imagine the black-market value?"

Jax nodded. "Billions, if he's to be believed." He pointed toward the door the owner of the coordinates had exited through. Chewing the contested piece of bacon, he leaned forward. "We can't let him sell that fleet to the empire."

Steve raised an eyebrow. "Who would you suggest we sell them to?"

Jax waved the reply away, "No, I mean we can't let him sell them to the empire. We most definitely can." He grinned, then continued. "Hey, listen. How about we keep this between us? I can cut you in 33 percent, even split with Naomi and me."

Steve leaned back, hands behind his head. "Or, I tell my brother, we beat you to the salvage, and he and I get 100 percent."

Jax made a face. "We have history..."

Steve rolled his eyes. "Please. Sex is great. Money is better." He grinned. "And you're not that good."

Jax frowned. "Fine. We'll do it as a group, four-way split."

Steve nodded slowly. "Deal." He pulled out his gPhone and pressed an icon. His brother answered. "Get dressed and knock on the door next door. We've got a job." He listened. "No, I don't know why you're naked. Of course, I didn't undress you, you perv. Yes, it'll be worth it. Don't forget Naomi." He put his gPhone down. "Think they can make the coffee less foul?"

Jax looked around. Most of the diner's patrons didn't seem to object to the black sludge the waitress was serving. "Doubt it."

Naomi and Marshall arrived a few minutes later. After being warned, the former ordered tea, the latter orange juice.

The bigger Delphino looked at his brother, then at Jax. "So?"

The server deposited the tea and orange juice and took the new arrivals' orders. Jax ordered an extra side of bacon to munch on. When the woman trundled off, he turned to Naomi and Marshall. "What do you know about the Nemesis Fleet?"

Marshall, sitting next to his brother, shrugged and elbowed the younger man. Steve replied, "I was here, dummy, I know where this is going." Marshall frowned.

Naomi sighed. "The Nemesis Fleet was supposed to be some last great hope of the Indies. A fleet of some of their newest designs." She looked at Marshall, who shrugged. "You need to read more. Anyway. They didn't have the crews for the ships yet, so they put droids on each ship, enough to skeleton crew them. They sent the fleet to a secret hiding place where it'd wait for the human crews to arrive."

Jax took over as the waitress delivered fresh plates of breakfast for Naomi and Marshall. He snatched one of the new pieces of bacon, crunching it, then said, "The battle of Zeus ended up taking place way ahead of schedule. It caught the Indies off-balance. They lost. It wasn't just a defeat—just about everyone in the military command structure was killed. The civilian leadership surrendered, but none of them knew where the fleet was." He took another bite. "Their coffee sucks, but the bacon is good. Anyhow, the Empire spent a few years looking, but space is big, and the fleet could have literally been anywhere."

Marshall nodded. "Neat. So?"

Jax shook his head, looked at Steve. "Not too late."

The other man shook his head in return and made a *go on* motion.

Jax sighed. "So..." he drawled. "We're gonna steal the location of the Nemesis Fleet, go find it, and hopefully, salvage it."

Marshall leaned forward, his grin revealing the piece of chive stuck in his teeth. "Why didn't you just say that?"

PART TWO

CHAPTER 5

After Naomi and Marshall finished breakfast and the impromptu band of rogues had ironed out the basics of their scheme, they left the diner in search of a transit line that got them to Dome 7, where their mark's ship was docked.

It turned out that Dome 7 was not actually closer to Dome 2 than their landing pad in Dome 18 was. Unlike Dome 18, there wasn't a direct transit line connecting their current location to Dome 7.

"I guess all landing domes are dingy on this planet," Naomi observed as they left the transit platform, walking into the main reception area of the spaceport. Several nearby trash bins were overflowing, and it looked like a small enclave of unhoused folks had set up a camp in one corner.

The group made its way through the welcome area and out into the dome proper. As in other spaceports, someone had painted safe walking paths onto the permacrete. They made their way across the three-kilometer-wide dome to Pad 15, two away from their target.

"That's an ugly ship," Marshall said from the pile of equipment the group was standing near, trying to look like they belonged there. The *Albright* was where her owner said she would be, all squat, boxy bulk freighter tonnage of her. The boarding ramp was, as expected, raised.

From behind them a voice said, "This place is a dump. Someone thought I was a trash bin and tried to pry my head off."

Naomi turned. "Hey, Rudy."

"I had to take two trains to get here," the droid continued.

Jax looked over his shoulder. "I don't know how you make it through the day." He pointed to the *Albright*. "That's our target."

"Why would you want to steal that scow?" the rust-colored navigation droid asked.

Jax made a face. "What? No, we're not stealing it. We're robbing it."

Rudy's flat head spun in a full circle. "Ah, that makes sense." His primary optical sensor settled on the *Albright*. "That model might have an intelligence aboard. Probably a dumb one, but still."

Marshall groaned. "More smart-mouthed starships. Great."

Rudy ignored the comment. "Wait here." His optical sensor turned to Naomi. "Come on." He rolled over to the ship, Naomi in tow.

Marshall watched them go, then turned to Jax. "What're they gonna do?"

Jax rubbed his chin. "Naomi knows her way around...computers."

At the *Albright*, Naomi looked around. "I need a data line."

"I know that," Rudy replied. He rolled to the starboard forward landing strut and pointed. There was an auxiliary access panel tucked in between two pieces of equipment.

Naomi tilted her head. "Okay, then." She walked over and placed a hand on the panel, her bio-circuitry pulsing as she pushed and pulled data from the ship's computer. She looked down at Rudy. "You're right. There's an SI."

"An SI? You're sure?" The look Naomi gave the droid was answer enough. "I wouldn't expect a ship like this to have something so advanced." Naomi nodded.

The boarding ramp lowered with a thud. Naomi waved the others over as she and Rudy headed up into the bulk freighter, *Albright*.

"Please stop right there," the overhead speaker said.

Naomi looked up at a camera pickup. "I'm afraid not." The others came up the ramp. "We should hurry."

"I have summoned the authorities," the ship said.

Naomi smirked. "No, you haven't. I'm pretty sure your boss has plenty of things on this ship that he wouldn't want the authorities to see." She grinned when no reply came.

Jax looked around the boarding area. He turned to the team. "Steve, bridge. Marshall and me, crew quarters. Naomi and Rudy, engineering and computer core." Nods all around.

"Please leave," the ceiling pleaded.

"Sorry," Naomi said.

"Okay, this is just gross," Naomi said, taking in the engineering compartment of the *Albright*.

"Captain Abano has many positive qualities. Cleanliness is not one of them," the ship's SI replied.

Rudy rolled over to a data port. "You won't do something silly like try to overload this data port, right?"

"No promises," the ceiling replied.

Naomi shook her head. "How did Captain—what was it?"

"Abano."

"Abano, get an SI installed on an absolute piece of shit like this?"

A hatch slid open, revealing the *Albright*'s computer core. The ceiling speaker said, "He won me in a bet."

"Lucky you." Rudy plugged into the data port.

"It has been...an experience," the ceiling said.

Naomi peeked into the much-too-small and also filthy computer closet. Abano or someone else had welded processing core racks to the bulkheads. Wiring ran all over the cramped space.

She placed a hand on the nearest processing core, her bio-circuits glowing.

"How are you doing that?" the ceiling speaker asked. When she didn't answer, it said, "I do not understand how a human can sift so much data, so rapidly."

She smiled. "I'm an enigma." She focused on the data streaming through her. Plenty of porn and other things she would later try to drink away the memories of. But no secret locations of legendary fleets.

From outside the cramped space, Rudy said, "I have had no luck."

She stepped back out into the main engineering area and looked at Rudy, then the camera. "Here's the deal. We don't want the ship. We want information."

The bridge of the *Albright* was not too dissimilar to the *Buttercup*'s. Steve made his way around the space. He and Jax had only seen the captain, and judging by the look of the bridge, the man didn't run with a crew very often. He appeared to have re-wired most of the consoles into a makeshift main panel epoxied next to the pilot's station.

"This guy is a piece of work," Steve said to no one.

"He is a far better man than the one who previously owned my processing cores," the ceiling replied.

Steve jumped. "Christ," he hissed. He looked around until he spotted the camera haphazardly mounted to the corner of the ceiling. "Don't sneak up people."

"I have no body and technically you are inside me."

"Thanks for that. So, your boss, he works solo?"

"When he can. There was a crew with us several months ago. I do not know what became of them."

"I know what happened to them. Why hasn't he hired on anyone since?" Steve dropped into the pilot's seat, looking over the console and its sloppily welded on cousin.

"He...He...I do not know. I assume he simply prefers to be alone." When Steve said nothing, the SI pressed. "Why are you here?"

"Your boss has something we want."

"What?"

"The location of the Nemesis Fleet. Do you know where it is?"

"I do not," the ship replied.

"He apparently found it less than a year ago. You weren't installed back then?"

"I was."

Steve turned to look over his shoulder at the camera, eyebrow arched.

"Captain Abano erased all navigational data as well as my core memories of the days before, during, and after his discovery. It is all a blank. He said it was for my own good."

"Great," Steve growled.

"You do not mean myself or the captain any harm?" the ceiling asked.

Naomi looked at Rudy, still plugged into the data terminal. She turned back to the ceiling and said, "Nope. We just want the data."

"Data about the Nemesis Fleet?"

Rudy's head spun to look at Naomi, who shrugged and said, "Yeah."

"I do not have it."

Rudy unplugged from the data port. "What do you mean?"

The ceiling was silent, then said, "I do not possess the location or navigational data as pertains to the Nemesis Fleet."

"That doesn't make any sense," Naomi said, more to herself.

"That is immaterial," the ship replied.

"I wasn't talking to you, but...what happened to the data?"

"The captain erased it all."

Rudy rolled in a slow circle. "How is he trying to sell it if he deleted it?"

"I do not know."

The *Albright* had four crew berths. Three were small double-bunk affairs, common on just about every freighter flying since the dawn of space flight. The first room was empty. The bunks did not even have mattresses. The captain had, at some point in the past, decided to use it as his storage room. Stuff that did not warrant being in the cargo hold, but also wasn't important or valuable enough to be in his quarters, had been piled up on the bunk frames and in the corners of the room.

"This guy is a bit of a pack rat," Marshall said as he and Jax crossed the corridor to the next crew berth. This one was identical in size to the one they just left, except that it had at some point been occupied. Swaths of satin had been draped across the upper bunk, creating a private area for the lower bunk. Beads and other decorations were affixed to the walls.

"What, the, hell?" Jax said. He looked at the ceiling. "I thought your captain traveled solo?"

"He does."

"So..." Jax looked at the camera in the room's corner, angled so that it could not see the beds. He also noticed for the first time that there was a small piece of fabric atop the camera, one that could be pulled down to obscure the entire room from view. He made a show of turning a slow circle in the middle of the room.

"He occasionally has visitors. One, in particular, travels with us often," the ceiling replied.

"A hooker," Marshall offered as he lifted the upper mattress to look underneath it. He none too gently pulled several photos and other things out from under the thin mattress, tossing them to the deck.

Jax looked at him. "Dude, really?"

"What?"

"Do we call you a goomba?"

"Probably."

Jax made a face. "Okay, fair. But it's insulting to use 'hooker.' Sex work is work, and she, whoever she is, doesn't need your judgy ass looking down on her."

"She's not here, you know," Marshall said, turning to look down at his room searching companion. "Defending her honor won't get you into her pants."

Jax made a rude gesture. "I'll start in the captain's quarters. You take the other, then meet up."

The captain's berth was pretty much what Jax expected, having seen the rest of the ship. A bunk, unmade. Stacks of boxes in the corners, parts from repairs lying on the deck, and the small desk turned into a repair station.

The room was about twice the size of the other berths, with just the single bunk, desk, and private head.

Jax kneeled down and looked under the desk. "Guessing what we want is in the safe."

"Are you speaking to me?" the ceiling asked.

Jax looked up and around the ceiling. No camera. "No, I

wasn't. Unless you can confirm that what we're looking for is in there." He pointed to the safe.

Naomi appeared in the doorway, Rudy squeezing past her, his roller ball squeaking on the floor.

Jax pointed. "Get to work."

Rudy said nothing.

Naomi said, "Nothing in the main computer. I did confirm that our friend here called his boss."

"How long?" Jax said.

She shrugged. "And that there was nothing that looked or felt like what we want. The main computer, the navigation buffer and sub-system...I even looked in the comm buffer and his porn stash. Nothing."

Marshall and Steve appeared behind Naomi, who moved into the captain's berth to make room.

Jax looked at Rudy, whose tiny metal fingers were a blur on the safe's keypad. "Guess it's in there."

Marshall looked past Jax to the safe. "We gotta hurry."

"If what you're looking for is as valuable as you say, it is not in the safe," the ship's managing Sapient Intelligence said.

Everyone looked up at the ceiling. What felt like a lifetime passed before the SI said, "Toilet."

Marshall and Steve were nearest the small head. The bigger Delphino spun and looked into the small restroom. He turned to look at the others. "Nope." He held both hands up.

"Don't be a baby!" Jax snapped. "Go put your hand in the toilet!"

Marshall glared and turned back to the toilet. A toilet that looked like the last time it was cleaned was when the ship rolled off the assembly line.

Jax turned to Steve. "You and Naomi go watch the front door." He turned to Rudy. "You too, Rudy."

Rudy rolled over next to Jax. "Baxter is on his way. I called him, just in case."

Jax nodded. "Good idea."

Marshall, on his knees, one arm buried in the toilet bowl up to his elbow, said, "I don't feel anything." He looked at Jax. "There's nothing in here."

"I meant the tank," the ship's SI said.

Naomi and Steve stepped off the boarding ramp of the *Albright* and came face to face with Baxter. "Hi," the matte black combat droid said. "You have company." He turned and pointed toward a group of people near the main entry to the spaceport section of the dome. The group looked mighty angry and was led by Captain Abano.

"Well, shit," Steve said. He had a blaster pistol on his hip, same as Naomi and the others. The group approaching them was equally armed.

Rudy rolled down the ramp. "I'm trying to see if I can find us an exit."

The group at the spaceport perimeter turned and marched straight for the *Albright*. Baxter walked to a nearby equipment cart that someone had left after working on the ugly freighter the team was robbing.

The group, a mix of spacers and what appeared to be ground crew, didn't waste any time with discussion. They opened fire.

"What the hell?" Naomi shouted, dropping to the ground

and crawling behind the boarding ramp. "They just started shooting!"

Steve joined Baxter behind the metal tool cart. He stood and returned fire, then crouched back down. "Right? And who are the other folks? Why are they shooting?"

Jax and Marshall were the last to come down the ramp, the former already firing as he joined Naomi behind the ramp. "I can't leave you all alone for a second."

Before anyone could reply, the sound of Baxter's weapons opening up barked through the space. Railgun rounds chewed up the permacrete. The big droid was trying to avoid killing the random assortment of attackers.

Steve looked at his brother. "You smell." He looked at Jax, who grinned. Then he winced as his brother punched him in the shoulder.

Baxter turned. "Less banter, more figuring out our escape." A powerful blast struck the droid in the chest, forcing him to take several steps back. He turned to the man holding a powerful-looking rifle. "That hurt." The man, or at least the top half of him, exploded in a fine mist as a railgun round tore through him. Baxter put a hand to his torso, sparks erupting from the damage he just sustained.

The attacking crowd paused for a moment. The team all turned to Baxter, who had kneeled behind the tool cart again. His swishing red optical sensor turned to the others. "What? It did hurt."

Rudy said. "I have found an exit. Two, rather." Everyone's gPhones beeped.

The cease fire ended as abruptly as it had begun as others from nearby ships opened fire, as well, assuming Jax and the others were ship thieves. Steve moved to get cover from a pair of women coming in from the side, each with wicked-looking pistols in both hands. "Why are new people shooting? They're not involved!" He squeezed off a shot before flattening himself to the oil stained permacrete. One of the women let out a pained howl, but the other produced an even more wicked-looking long gun from the inside of her dark brown long coat.

Baxter spun his upper torso but stopped suddenly, frozen. A pair of glancing shots from the captain of the *Albright* caught him in the torso, knocking him over.

Jax pulled his gPhone out and looked at the data Rudy sent, then his damaged mechanical friend. "Let's go! Steve and Marshmallow, take the exit Rudy marked, B. Naomi and I will take A. We'll regroup at the ship!"

Marshall stood and fired, then said, "Why do we have to go through the sewer?"

Jax shot a man in the knee then said, "Because you already smell like one." He motioned to the two brothers. "Go!"

Marshall made a rude gesture, then grabbed his brother's collar, hauling him up. The two crawled toward the indicated sewer grate, while Jax and Naomi covered them. Baxter got to his feet and opened fire, as well.

Jax shouted, "Droids, go!"

Baxter turned and found Rudy. He didn't protest or wait, snatching the much smaller droid under one arm and sprinting for the service airlock in the far dome wall.

Jax crawled to the tool cart, then stood and laid down a stream of energy bolts. He didn't hit anyone, but the sparks and damage he inflicted on other tool carts and pieces of equipment kept everyone opposite him down.

Before everyone could start returning fire, he started toward the next nearest cart for cover. He stood and fired again as Naomi followed him, firing her own weapon haphazardly.

They reached the dome wall and a narrow service hatch.

Two shots from Jax's pistol took care of the locking mechanism. He looked past Naomi as she slipped into the service corridor. He opened fire on the few pursuers that were still actually pursuing them. Most of their attackers seemed to have gotten bored once the return fire had diminished.

CHAPTER 6

Baxter was running from dome to dome, following the curving walls and transit tunnels. The atmosphere of Del Rio Two wasn't hospitable to humans, but it didn't bother droids. He rounded a corner and caught his foot on a rock, nearly losing his footing.

Rudy used lower-powered comms to say, *Are you okay?*

The combat droid didn't physically react, but sent back, *Like, existentially?*

No, physically. That rifle looked like it did some serious damage. I've never seen you trip before.

It did, Baxter replied. *Several internal systems are damaged and degrading.* He made a quick turn to follow a conduit of some kind that branched off the transit tunnel he was following.

Rudy said, *You do know where you're going...Right?*

Baxter nodded once. *Yes. Stop bothering me.* His pace quickened.

The service tunnel was inside the dome wall, following the kilometers' wide arc. When they stopped at another narrow hatch, Jax said, "This should open up in the main reception area. As long as we don't attract the attention of station person-nel, we can just walk in."

"Oh, that all?" Naomi frowned. She put a hand on the simple locking mechanism. The bio-circuit tattoos on her hand pulsed once. The hatch swung out on hinges that hadn't been oiled, possibly ever. Despite the noise, no one turned to look at the pair exiting the service corridor.

Jax looked at the monitor displaying transit routes that Dome 7 was part of. He pointed. "Looks like we need that line, blue. Change trains at Dome 4, then straight to our dome."

She nodded, pointing to a platform. "There."

The wait wasn't long. For all its dingy lawlessness, Del Rio Two had an incredibly efficient transit system.

Dome 4 was one of the agricultural domes. About half the size of a spaceport dome, the entire floor was row after row of a mix of hydroponic and real soil growth bins thirty stories tall.

"All this...you'd think someone would have planted some coffee," Jax said. They were standing on the transit platform, waiting for their connection. Technicians were minding the various bins. He shuddered, remembering the horrid sludge that the diner from breakfast tried to pass off as coffee.

Naomi shrugged. "Maybe you just picked a shithole?"

Jax hunched his shoulders. "Possible."

The train arrived, announced by two soft chimes.

"Next stop, Nemesis Fleet," Jax said.

As the transit car slid away from the station toward Dome 7 and the waiting *Osprey*, Naomi said, "You just gonna jinx it like that?"

Dome 7 and the *Osprey* were exactly as they left them. From what Jax could tell, he and Naomi had arrived first. He pointed to the lift that would take them up to the second tier of docking pads.

Jax's gPhone beeped. He looked at the screen, then craned

his neck to look around the dome. He pointed. "The boys are here."

Naomi turned. "Which boys?"

"The mechanical ones," Jax said. He put his phone to his ear. "Skip, yeah, get the pre-flight started and departure clearance." He pulled the device away from his ear, tapped an icon, then put it back. "Hurry up."

Naomi looked at him. "What're you doing?"

Jax smiled. "What do you mean?"

The lift rattled to a stop, gate sliding open. They started toward the *Osprey*.

"I mean, it's going to take the Delphinos a while to get here."

Jax fished the plastic wrapped data storage unit from a pocket. "Sucks to be them."

"You're going to leave them here. They're never going to forgive you."

Walking up the *Osprey*'s boarding ramp, Jax looked over his shoulder. "I didn't think I'd ever forgive them for how they treated me in school, but I did. They'll get over it." He continued up the spiral staircase that connected the three main decks of the Valerian Coop Infiltrator. "All's fair in love and larceny."

Naomi was following Jax up to the bridge, shaking her head. "Skip, I want to be on the record as being against leaving the Delphinos."

The ceiling speaker replied, "Okay, but I do not think they would consider me an unbiased system of record."

Naomi dropped into the station she used when on the bridge. "True." She looked forward. "You're sure?"

Jax was working through the pre-flight when Rudy zipped up the hollow center of the staircase. "You're leaving the Delphinos behind? That's going to piss them off."

Jax flipped a few switches. "Almost certainly. Skip, we ready?"

"We have received clearance to depart."

Jax powered up the lift engines. As the *Osprey* rose, her landing gear folded up with a metallic groan. The soft clang of hull panels closing over the stowed gear signified the ship's readiness to depart. Jax guided the nimble ship out of the dome and up and out of the atmosphere.

An hour later, the Delphino brothers stepped off the transit car to the obvious relief of the other riders.

"I can't believe we had to crawl through the sewers," Marshall groused.

They walked through the reception area into the main spaceport facility.

"At least the rest of you smells like your arm," his brother quipped, then juked out of range of a shoulder punch.

They walked around the dome wall to the lift and took it to the next tier.

They had walked a few dozen meters when Steve hissed, "That asshole."

"What?" Marshall asked, looking up from whatever he was busying himself with. "Hey, isn't that the pad—"

"That the *Osprey* was on? Yeah. That dick left us," Steve said.

"I'll kill him," Marshall said.

"Not if I kill you first," someone said. Both Delphinos turned to see Captain Marcus Abano of the *Albright*. "You stole something from me."

It turned out that Captain Abano, while being extremely cautious about his find falling into the wrong hands, didn't bother to encrypt the data storage module. Naomi had the coordinates before the *Osprey* had even reached safe wormhole distance from Del Rio Two.

Unfortunately, the un-encrypted drive had only contained a single data file: a set of spatial coordinates.

The *Osprey* emerged from its wormhole in the Gibson system.

"Now what?" Naomi asked. "We can't search the entire planet."

They were in high orbit over a mottled blue and brown planet.

"Nor would you want to," Skip said. "This planet, LV-426, is a dead world. The terraforming equipment malfunctioned well into the process. The atmosphere turned semi-toxic fast, forcing the entire colony to evacuate. It was originally named Cornucopia, but when it failed, they reduced it to its cosmic catalog ID."

Rudy raised a thin metallic arm. "What was the name on

the data file?"

"Name?" Jax asked.

"The file name," Rudy clarified, sounding annoyed.

Naomi said, "The Rose."

Rudy bobbed on his smart material ball, his computer interface jack spinning and whirring. "The name of the primary city for this colony is…"

"Rose City," the ship's SI filled in.

Rudy beeped. "Got it in one."

Naomi nodded. "Makes sense. He was careful to not leave the data in plain sight, but didn't want to take a chance he might lose or forget something." She sighed. "This is going to be a goddamned scavenger hunt."

Jax grunted. "Yeah, this doesn't seem as straightforward as it did yesterday." He consulted the flight console. "Don't suppose we know the coordinates of Rose City or its spaceport?"

Skip answered, "Based on data from the Internex at the time the colony collapsed, there were only a few large cities." Jax's console lit up. "I've narrowed it down to these two cities."

Jax adjusted their course. "Okay, we'll do a speedy orbit, find the city that most closely matches your data, and get down there."

Rudy disconnected from his console. "I'll be back." He dropped from the bridge deck before either Jax or Naomi could reply.

Jax looked over his shoulder. "What's he up to?"

"Not a droid whisperer," Naomi replied. She pointed at Jax's console. "Find us our next stop."

Rudy rolled into engineering to see Baxter standing in his charging cradle. *Were you able to make repairs?* he beamed.

The combat droid looked completely shut down.

Baxter?

The scatter light on the front of Baxter's head sprung to life, swishing back and forth. *Sorry. Self-repair system is doing all it can.*

Skip said, *What can we do?*

Unknown. I'm running a diagnostic, but it is slow going, the combat droid replied.

Rudy bobbed up and down on his smart material roller-ball. *I've started a search for replacement parts, but they're getting pretty hard to find.* He turned and rolled out of engineering.

Jax turned. "I think I've got it." He pointed to his nav console. The familiar ring of a spaceport sat in the center.

Naomi stood and moved to his pilot station, leaning over Jax's shoulder. On one display was the planetary scanner read-out. Terrain details were filling in as the *Osprey* flew past overhead.

Jax scrolled back through the data and zoomed in on a section near the coast of one of the largest oceans on the planet. Most of the city lay in ruins, towers fallen over, buildings gutted. The spaceport ring was partially collapsed and overgrown with native plants. Nature had made quick work of the colony once the human occupants left.

Naomi nodded. "That's gotta be it." She moved back to her station.

The *Osprey* tilted, the view of space beyond flashing by until the entire forward view was the planet LV-426. A few wispy clouds were drifting through the upper atmosphere as the nimble infiltrator dropped toward the surface.

"Guess I don't need to check for landing clearance," Jax said, banking the *Osprey* as he reduced speed.

Debris from the collapsed ring wall littered one section of the spaceport landing area. Opposite the damaged section was a remarkably clean area larger than the *Osprey* would need to land, but just about the right size for a ship the size of Captain Abano's *Albright*.

Jax and Naomi stepped off the staircase in the main cargo hold above the small embarkation room. Jax looked around. "Hey, Baxter?"

The cargo hold took up the entire deck except for a small med bay and the engineering compartment at the rear. The reinforced hatch to engineering slid open, and Baxter walked out. The damage to his torso was no longer visible.

Jax tilted his head. "All fixed up?" He pointed to Baxter's torso. The armor was good as new.

"Good as new," the combat droid said. The armor was easy to repair. Jax had stolen the industrial replicator recipe for Mark IX combat droid armor several years ago. Baxter could print the pieces on the type 3 fabricator tucked in a corner of engineering any time he needed.

Jax smiled. "Can't keep my pal Baxter down." He turned back to the staircase. "We'll need breathers, but according to Skip, that's it. No acid air or anything like that."

"Oh, lucky us," Naomi quipped.

Even the cleared off portion of the spaceport was in obvious disrepair. The permacrete was cracked, and small plants with delicate-looking purple flowers had pushed through almost every crack, widening them further.

Naomi looked around as she stepped off the boarding ramp. "Okay, so...now what?"

Baxter pointed toward the administrative section of the ring wall. It appeared to be intact, at least more so than the rest of the facility.

Jax looked. "Why?"

The combat droid shrugged. "It's the nearest facility that is intact. I can't imagine that pudgy captain would trek very far with his secrets. Or possessed the needed skills or interest to rehab any of this." He motioned to the rest of the spaceport.

Naomi turned and started toward the admin center. "Good a guess as any," she said over her shoulder.

Baxter and Jax fell in behind her. The former said, "I don't guess."

The administrative center looked like any other you'd find on any of countless colonized worlds. The ground floor comprised customs windows and a waiting room, plus a few assorted offices for the lower-level spaceport managers. The upper floors were all offices and conference rooms.

Near the exit was an alcove with a single desk in it, protected by blaster proof transparent titanium the same grade as starship viewports. The currency exchange.

The years of neglect were obvious. Plants of all kinds had found their way into the offices and rooms of the administrative center. A particularly aggressive vine had torn wall panels off as it climbed. Several posters for a place called Tulip Acres were in various stages of rotting off of the walls.

Baxter's swishing scatter light took in the space. "Look." He was pointing toward the currency exchange.

Naomi stepped into the small office, big enough only for the exchange officer and a client. She looked back to Baxter. "What am I looking at?"

Baxter pointed to the floor. The purple-flowered weeds had worked their way up through the floor, ripping apart the perma-crete—except that there were several plants that had been trampled around the entrance to the small workspace.

Naomi's eyebrows rose. "Look at you, investigator Baxter." The droid inclined his head. She dropped into the chair and noticed the distinct lack of dust cloud. She looked up at Baxter, then Jax, smiling.

They tore the small workspace apart. There wasn't much to work with in the first place, just the small desk and two chairs.

"Nothing," Jax said.

Naomi snapped her fingers. "The vault." When Jax looked at her askance, she said, "The currency exchange has a vault on the third floor. I bet our friend is making use of it."

Jax looked around. "How? From here?"

Naomi moved a hand to a small panel in the wall. It slid open to reveal what looked like a pneumatic tube system.

Jax looked at the set of tubes. "Okay, next stop, third floor." He pointed to the door that led to the stairwell.

"Of course," Jax said when he pushed open the door to the service stairs. The metal stairs had rusted through and collapsed. The vines that were doing their best to pull down the walls in the main area had already succeeded at taking over the stairwell. Dark green with white flowers, the vines had destroyed the stairwell all the way up to the third floor, leaving nothing but twisted, rusted metal.

"Guess we climb," Jax said, looking at the vine-covered walls and the remnants of stars. "If it could pull down stairs, guessing it can hold us." He looked at Baxter. "You better stay put."

"Agreed," the droid said.

Jax looked at Naomi, who said, "By all means, you first."

He sighed and grabbed a handful of vines, pulling himself up. "Sticky," he complained.

Naomi waited until Jax was a few feet off the ground before following him. The vines were thick and actually felt like a sticky rope in her hands. She could see how these things did so much damage.

Jax had reached the third floor and was working his way around the shaft toward the remains of the landing.

Naomi grabbed her next handhold and felt the vine shift. She stopped and looked around, waiting to see if some section of the plant had come loose from the wall or if Jax had fallen to his death. Nothing happened. He was still making his way up. She pulled herself up, and the vine shuddered again, this time wriggling in her grasp. She let out a shriek and released the vine. With her other hand, she held on as she swung sideways.

"What's wrong?" Jax looked down.

"The vine. It...it moved."

"Go on a diet." He kept working his way toward the door to the third level.

Naomi made a face. "That's not what I mean, asshole. I think the vine is—" The sound of crumbling permacrete filled the stairwell shaft, followed by a wet smacking sound that came from multiple directions at once. Several of the larger flowers along the lengths of vine moved, the petals waving and slapping against each other. The center of each opened to reveal a mouth. "Alive," she finished.

The entire stairwell shaft seemed to come alive at the same time; vines writhed and pulled from the wall. White flowers that moments before were pretty, were now horrific things, mouths opening and closing in anticipation of a meal.

Jax let go of a section of vine, trying to swing closer to the landing only to have the vine he was still holding onto shift further from his destination. "Damnit!" He pulled his blaster from its holster and fired at the vine. The blast scorched the plant, causing several of the nearby flowers to make a pained keening sound.

From above him, a flower much larger than the others snaked down toward Jax. Each petal was at least as long as his forearm and ended in a hardened, spike-like structure. The petals flexed, designed to clutch prey and pull it toward its central mouth structure. The center of the flower was a gaping maw lined with needle-like teeth.

Jax screamed and took aim. His first few shots went wide as the vines he was clinging to shook and slithered. One of the smaller flowers clamped onto his hand, drawing blood and another scream.

Naomi scrambled up closer to Jax and the third-floor landing before pulling her own pistol free of its holster. "This is so gross!" she shouted, firing into the vine near the flower still latched onto Jax's hand. A vine snaked out from the wall, wrapping itself around her leg. She screamed and let go of the vine she was clutching.

The large flower was much closer to Jax now, and the vine it had sprouted from was as thick as his arm. The needle-like teeth were making a grating noise as the mouth opened and closed.

"What are you two..." Baxter said, stepping back into the shaft. His combat blades extending, metal clicking into place. "I can't leave you alone for a minute." He went to work, his blades slashing vine and permacrete alike. The flesh-eating flowers wailed in unison.

The large flower turned toward Baxter, its vine creaking as it slithered lower, toward the attacking combat droid.

Jax holstered his pistol and scrambled toward the third-floor landing. Once he had a firm grip on a piece of the metal landing, he pulled his pistol and opened fire on the vines. The large flower turned to him, and he shot it. A lot. The flower burst into flames with a wet gurgle. Petals drifted to the floor. "Naomi!" he shouted. He waved her toward him.

She scrambled along the writhing mass of vines, doing her best to avoid the tiny snapping jaws of the flowers.

Baxter looked up. Purple plant juice covered him, his optic sensor swishing back and forth through the muck. His blades disengaged, folding back into his arms to be replaced by his blasters. "Get moving."

Jax pulled Naomi up onto the landing. "Good times." She nodded, panting.

Below, the surviving vines were writhing all over, flower mouths biting air. Baxter stepped back out into the main administrative offices. "This is disgusting."

CHAPTER 7

The third floor of the administrative section was in just as much disrepair as the first. The vines that they now knew were carnivorous and hungry had penetrated the walls, floor, and ceiling, pulling the rooms apart slowly but surely. Duracrete chunks littered the area.

"Know where the vault is?" Jax asked.

"Why would I know that?" Naomi replied, making a slow circle. She stopped and pointed. "Guessing there, though." She was pointing at a doorway with an intact door. She looked at the floor, tapping a hand against her thigh. "Yeah, that feels like it lines up, more or less."

Jax nodded. "Plus, you know, door on its hinges still. Definitely a bit suspicious."

The room beyond the door was as relatively clean as the door. Clearly, Captain Abano spent some time making sure his hiding place was secure, even if that meant it stood out like a sore thumb. In the center of the far wall was a vault door in near-pristine condition. Above it, a tattered sign read, *Lock Vault at End of Shift.*

Jax's gPhone beeped. He tapped his earpiece. "Yeah?"

"Captain. We have company," Skip said.

Naomi kneeled next to the vault door control panel, resting both hands on it.

Jax watched her, then said, "Company? What?"

"The *Albright*," Rudy offered. He was aboard the *Osprey* still.

"Knew we should have sabotaged that thing," Jax hissed. He looked over Naomi's shoulder. "How's it going?"

She looked up. "Leave me alone." Her eyes closed again.

Jax looked around the room. Whatever furniture had been in the room was long gone. Captain Abano must have cleared it all out. Nothing to use as cover or barricade the door with. He tapped his ear. "Baxter, you still downstairs?"

"Yes."

"Go set up somewhere. We may need cover."

"Copy that."

Jax walked out into the hallway. It looked intact as far as he could see, the gentle bend that followed the curve of the space-port vanishing in the distance.

"Oh, this is interesting," Rudy said over the team comms.

"What?" Jax asked, pacing and trying his best to not bug Naomi while she worked.

"The lone wolf, Captain Abano, seems to have hired a pack. He has six men with him. Sorry, seven. Well-armed men," the nav droid said. "They look mean."

"How is that interesting?" Jax demanded.

"Interesting to me," Rudy replied.

Jax's gPhone beeped. He looked at the photo that Skip just sent. "Abano's friend from the diner."

Rudy continued, "Yeah, they're mad. Lots of pointing at the *Osprey* and gesticulating. I wish I had lip reading software installed."

"Dude..." Jax said.

"Oh, they're heading your way. Looks like they know exactly where you are."

Jax sighed, looking at the ceiling. "Well, yeah. We're in Abano's hiding place. Bax, can you keep 'em busy?"

"Roger," the combat droid replied.

"Got it!" Naomi shouted from the room behind Jax.

Jax went back into the vault room. His partner was sitting on the ground, her jet-black hair matted to her forehead. She scooted back so he could open the door to the vault wide enough to step inside.

"Know what you're looking for?" Naomi asked from outside.

Jax leaned out of the vault, holding another data module. "Only thing in there."

"He set up this whole secret hideout, just for that?" Naomi said, shaking her head. The expense Abano must have gone to in order to clean up and refurbish the vault couldn't have been insignificant. "I kind of assumed this was his secret lair. You really think this whole thing is on the up and up?"

"Scavenger hunt," Naomi continued, getting to her feet.

Jax shoved the data module into the waistband of his pants. "I mean, like you said...This whole secret lair thing, and all that's here is this?" He tapped the data module. "Certainly leads me to think he's pretty damn sure about the fleet."

"He'd better be, all this treasure hunt crap," Naomi groused.

The sound of Baxter's arm blasters firing snapped Jax and Naomi's heads toward the stairwell. "Time to go," they said to each other.

Jax moved to a window that looked into the spaceport. He could see the two starships parked in the distance. Nearer, he could see six armed thugs and Captain Abano crouching behind debris and abandoned pieces of equipment firing toward the ring wall. *Where was the seventh guy?* Baxter was down there, somewhere out of Jax's line of sight. The combat droid's weapons fire was very much in sight. Energy bolts flew in both directions.

Down on the ground floor, Baxter had his forearm blasters deployed and was keeping the gunmen busy. He had intended to deploy his railguns, but something went wrong.

His operating system was throwing alerts one after the next:

Railgun servo-motors non-responsive.
Overload in Sub-Circuit Bravo Nine.
Sub-Processor Gamma Zero Zero Two One, offline.

Baxter kneeled down as return fire stitched the outside of the administrative building where he had been standing a moment ago.

Secondary sub-processor assembly registering uneven power flow.
Locomotion routines corrupted. Self-repair initiated.

Baxter stopped firing. The gunmen rushed into the entry and stopped short. One of them walked up to the inert combat droid. "Think it's dead?"

Abano scoffed. "It's a droid, you idiot. An old one. Guessing its age caught up with it." He walked up to Baxter and shoved, tipping the kneeling matte black droid over. He nodded further into the complex. "There's a stairwell this way. Come on."

When Jax lost contact with Baxter, he swore. "Abano's gotta have a way up here that isn't climbing the man-eating vines." Naomi nodded. "These places all have a similar layout." He looked around, then pointed. "Come on."

Spaceports have had more or less the same layout since humans left Earth. A permacrete ring, usually four kilometers in diameter, three or four stories high. The ground floors are usually mechanical bays and storage units rented by repair and shipping companies. The only way in or out is the main administrative section and its customs checkpoint, usually two, at opposite sides of the wide circle. The floors above are a mix: rental office space available to anyone who wants to be near incoming and outgoing ships, administrative facilities, sometimes some governmental offices.

Kramerica Industries occupied the second and third floors of the spaceport ring a few degrees to the right of the administrative complex. The main hallway ran the entire circumference of the spaceport, connecting the offices and lift bays. Without power, Naomi couldn't do her thing on the locking mechanisms of the connecting doors.

Jax's pistol, however, had no such issues. Walking into the abandoned office, he noticed row after row of low-walled cubicles filling the entire space, except the outer offices with their windows overlooking the spaceport.

"What do you think these people did?" Naomi asked, looking at a cubicle, her breath fogging her breather. "This colony wasn't standing for long, yet this company looks like it was up and running at full speed." She picked up a packet of paper, bound with a clip. The paper was yellowed, the outer pieces crumbled.

Jax lifted something off the desk he was standing next to, a plastic figurine with an oversized head. It was a character from an old vid. The paint on the head had chipped and faded. He tossed it on the ground. A cloud of dust erupted where it landed. "I'm sure it was importing, exporting, or both. Almost every business that sets up in a spaceport ring is one of those." He looked around the space. "These guys musta set up right when the colony settled."

A noise in the hallway they just left caused both of them to stop moving. Jax tilted his head the way they came, then turned and pointed to a door at the opposite end of the office space, likely a service door to a hallway between office spaces.

Naomi nodded and walked toward the far door, Jax on her tail. He whispered, "We should carry more guns."

She looked at him. "Or, we could try to get into fewer predicaments where we're shot at."

He passed Naomi and pushed open the door. "Where's the fun in that?" He grinned.

As Naomi walked through, a plasma bolt struck the door frame, eliciting an undignified shriek as she ducked.

I have lost contact with Baxter, Skip informed Rudy. The navigation droid was plugged into his station on the bridge, accessing the *Osprey*'s sensors and cameras.

Rudy disconnected. *Is he damaged? Destroyed?*

Unknown.

Rudy rolled to the stairwell and plummeted down to the small boarding room at the lowest level of the ship. The ramp dropped and unfolded.

Wish me luck, Rudy said, rolling down the ramp. The *Albright* was barely fifty meters away. Rudy rolled as fast as his smart material rollerball would allow toward the administrative building. *Scan the* Albright, *see if there is anything I can jimmy when I'm done.*

Copy, Skip replied. *Good luck.*

The uneven ground posed little difficulty for the rust-colored droid, his roller ball adjusting density and size to handle the broken and uneven permacrete with ease.

When Rudy reached Baxter, he found him frozen in a crouch, tipped over, leaning against the bent frame of a chair. Rudy rolled over and reached for the access panel tucked in the armor under Baxter's right arm.

It took a minute or two of tinkering before Baxter's optical sensor blinked to life. Rudy withdrew his small metal hand from inside his much larger friend. *Glad you're still functional, more or less*, he beamed as he rolled backward to give the combat droid room to get to its feet.

"Thanks." Baxter looked around. "Sit rep?"

Rudy bobbed up and down on his roller ball. "Jax and Naomi are still up there, somewhere. Your friends are up there, too."

Baxter looked around, then up at the ceiling. "I'm not going to be much use until I address this sub-processor damage." He put a metal hand on the section of his torso that had taken the shot earlier. Looking down at Rudy, he said, "Let's go make ourselves useful."

Jax dove through the doorway, turning as he fell to shoot blindly back into the abandoned Kramerica office. He heard someone scream as he hit the ground and kicked the door closed behind him. "See? This is fun, right?" He grinned as he stood up, offering a hand to his business partner. "Aren't you glad you forced your way into my life?" Naomi's expression was answer enough.

The door behind them splintered under a barrage of blaster fire. The door sagged, falling from its frame.

Jax and Naomi ducked. He shoved her toward the T-intersection connecting the service corridor to the main walkway that ran through the entire circle of the spaceport.

They turned and dashed past the door of the Seniram Coop, then Modular Combat Systems, Inc.

"Man, this spaceport's leasing office was aggressive," Jax said as they passed another office space that looked fully furnished. He turned to look over his shoulder as a man came into view. He squeezed off a few wild shots, sending the other man scrambling back out of sight.

"We gotta get off this floor," Naomi said as they jogged

around the bend. She skidded to a halt at another intersection, this one with a pair of elevator doors. She raced to the doors, putting a hand on the control panels. She shook her head and looked at Jax. "Dead."

He handed her his pistol and removed his multi-tool from a pocket in his vest. He jammed the blade between the doors and started prying them apart.

Naomi moved back to the corner. She swore and opened fire with both guns. Someone shouted, a pained sounding noise. She looked over her shoulder. "Got one." She ducked as several energy bolts struck the corner, sending plastic and plaster in all directions.

"Don't get cocky, kid," Jax replied as the doors slipped apart, revealing an empty shaft.

Naomi frowned. "Is that a line from one of those old vids?" She turned to their attackers and fired a few shots.

Jax leaned into the shaft, reaching for the emergency ladder. "Come on." He waved.

Naomi fired again and bolted from her corner. Jax made room for her on the ladder, accepting his blaster pistol as she worked her way down the ladder. Jax fired from the relative safety of the elevator shaft. Two men leaned out from cover, firing wildly. Jax swore and leaned further into the shaft.

"Come on!" Naomi hissed. She was on the ground floor, standing opposite the ladder.

Jax leaned back to the open doors and fired several rounds, forcing the attackers to scatter. There were four now. He holstered his pistol and put his feet against the ladder's side rails and loosened his grip. He shot down the ladder in a semi-controlled fall.

Naomi pulled her own pistol and fired toward the third-floor door, keeping their pursuers from poking their heads through.

Jax landed and started waving his hands. "Fuck! That hurts!" He blew on both hands, the palms bright red from the friction.

Naomi shook her head as she pulled the release on the inside of the doors, pushing them apart.

Rudy and Baxter were standing outside the *Albright*. The nav droid pointed to a cluster of maneuvering thrusters. "Destroy a few of those. The pre-flight won't let the ship launch without maneuvering thrusters."

Baxter nodded, deploying his arm blasters. He methodically walked around the dilapidated freighter, firing on and destroying clusters of thrust nozzles. "How many?"

Rudy rolled around a landing strut, stopping next to the combat droid. "Why not all of them?"

The elevator bay was designed to be an ornately decorated lobby space. The years and vines had made sure that no longer was the case. One of the lift doors was partly open. Jax leaned into look. He turned back Naomi. "No vines. Go figure."

"Really?" she asked. Vines were evident along several walls and a section of flooring opposite the door where they had exited into the lobby. She leaned into the shaft. "Huh."

Naomi leaned further into the dark space, grasping the service ladder. "Down we go," she said a second before loosening her grip and allowing herself to slide down the ladder, her feet outside the rungs.

A noise from the office space they had just fled came from the door. Jax jumped into the shaft behind her, mimicking her move to slide down the ladder.

The lift was sitting at the ground floor. By the time Jax landed, Naomi had the ceiling panel open and had jumped down into the empty car. He followed.

The elevator lobby on the ground floor was in worse shape than its third-floor sibling. Off to one side there was a corridor, partially collapsed ages ago, likely leading to the common hallway. The only other door was a large hatch labeled *Sanford and Son Scrap.*

Naomi pointed at the door for the scrap company. "Come on, action star." She pushed the doors apart with relative ease.

Sanford and Son was a mechanical bay. One large space, full of starship parts: engine components, life support equipment, hull panels, and vines—the same vines from the stairwell earlier, but more, a lot more. The lethal flowers filled the space.

"Oh, lovely. These things," Jax said.

A series of thuds came from the elevator shaft. Jax turned and pushed the doors to the mechanical bay closed. "Ideas?"

Naomi rushed further into the space, careful to not step on any of the vines that crisscrossed the floor. "Come on." She moved behind a large environmental processor, likely from a capital ship, based on its size. Jax followed just as the doors to the bay pushed open.

"They gotta be in here," a man said.

Jax looked at Naomi and whispered, "Now what?"

She pointed further back inside the space: rack upon rack of parts of all shapes and sizes. The racks had become a maze of vines and their carnivorous flowers.

"No damn way." Jax shook his head.

"Don't be a baby," Naomi hissed, pushing him toward the racks.

Another voice said, "What's with all these stupid vines?"

They reached the nearest rack, and Naomi shouted, "Hey dummies, we're back here!" Jax's eyes went wide. She pushed him toward the vine-strewn gap between two racks of parts. From the front of the shop, they heard the two men, and maybe one or two more, start stomping through the shop. Their pursuers weren't interested in stealth, knocking over stacks of junk in their haste.

"Move faster," Naomi hissed, pushing against Jax's back. He

sped up, crouching under a thick tangle of vines. His hand pressed on a vine, which immediately began squirming. He yelped. "But quietly," she added, pressing her hand on his backside. "Go."

"There!" one of the men shouted. A plasma bolt struck the rack over their heads, scorching several vines, waking up the nearby flowers.

"Go!" Naomi shouted, rising enough to run. Jax stood and scrambled diagonally from one section of racks to another, out of line of sight of their pursuers.

"This way, come on!" someone shouted. A rack shook as someone ran into it. "Damnit. Stupid vines."

Jax and Naomi scrambled through the vine-strewn canyons, doing their best to not wake or disturb the plants that were everywhere.

Naomi emerged from a cluster of vines and saw that there were no more racks. They had reached the back wall of the warehouse. She turned as Jax crawled out behind her.

He looked around. "Uh..." She shushed him, then turned to the rows of racks and accompanying vines. She pulled her pistol and fired a few carefully aimed shots as far into the mess of metal and plant as she could.

The sound of their pursuers struggling and shouting came from the unintentional jungle. Naomi turned to Jax, grinning. She whispered, "That'll keep this group busy." She pointed to the right and the outer wall of the parts shop. They crept along the wall, then followed the front wall as far as they could toward the door. The screams of their pursuers were still echoing through the Sanford and Son warehouse.

At the door, Jax turned and looked back into the space, bolts of energy occasionally lancing out in random directions, punctuated by more screams. "That was easier than I expected."

Naomi looked at him. "Unless I counted wrong, that isn't all of them."

Jax looked around. "Then let's get the hell out of here." He extended a hand toward the partially blocked intersection that led back to the main concourse for the ground level. The blockage at the entry to the corridor wasn't too big an obstacle, despite appearances. The pair was able to climb through in a matter of minutes. The rest of the corridor turned out to be in pretty good shape. Rounding a corner on their way into a wider shopping area and food hall, they came face to face with Captain Abano, the man he had been talking to on Del Rio Two, and three armed men. They didn't have the look of mercenaries, more like armed spacers in mismatched bits of armor and padding.

Naomi didn't hesitate, drawing her pistol and firing, mostly wildly, at Abano and his friends as she darted for cover.

"I know that guy!" the man who had eaten breakfast with Abano shouted before diving behind a dust covered table.

Jax blinked and followed his partner's lead, squeezing off a few shots as he ran sideways into the sea of tables and dusty vendor stalls.

"This way!" Naomi shouted, pointing toward a tall arched entryway that looked like it led to one of the wide public entryways and the spaceport landing area beyond.

Abano and his men returned fire, energy bolts ripping into stalls and tables all around them, leaving little scorch marks and fires. Deciding that speed was preferable, Naomi and Jax both put their hands over their heads and ran as fast as they could for the exit. Things were exploding all around them.

Reaching the exit, they burst through and didn't slow. "Skip!" Jax shouted after tapping his earpiece.

"Yes?"

"Get ready to go!"

CHAPTER 8

"Welcome ba—" Skip started to say as Jax and Naomi ran up the boarding ramp, the former slapping the control panel to raise the ramp as he passed.

"Prep for takeoff!" Jax shouted over him. He sprinted up the stairs as quickly as he could, taking them two at a time. His foot caught a stair, and he stumbled a few steps before the flight deck. "Shit!" he swore. Getting to his feet, he wiped his palms on his trousers and continued to the bridge.

Rudy was in the docking port at his station. "Welcome back."

Naomi reached the bridge as Jax was flipping switches. A blaster bolt struck the transparent viewscreen, leaving a faint gray smudge.

"We're being shot at," Skip said. Another blast struck the transparent titanium viewscreen, leaving another scorch mark, but otherwise causing no damage, the transparent material designed to resist blaster fire from ships.

Naomi dropped into the seat at her station. Jax said, "I see that. Deploy the anti-personnel weapons."

"Done," Skip said moments before the familiar whine of

blasters echoed through the ship. From small compartments in the wing roots, a pair of blasters dropped down on telescoping arms. Each blast spun, taking aim on their attackers, opening fire.

"Reactor is ready," Naomi reported.

Jax nodded but said nothing, his full attention on getting the *Osprey* ready to lift off. Technically, Skip could handle every aspect of flying the ship, but Jax had made it abundantly clear over the years that, whenever possible, he was the pilot. The pre-flight check was more or less complete before he sat down. He pushed the lift engine throttle up, easing the ship up off the broken permacrete.

The growl of the lift engines drowned out the whine of the anti-personnel blasters. They continued laying down fire until the ship was too high for them to be effective. Both blasters slid back into their compartments automatically.

"Captain, I'm detecting three ships in orbit," Skip announced as the *Osprey* gained altitude. Jax cut in the main thrusters, driving the ship forward, away from the spaceport and the angry freight hauler and his friends. A few pointless blaster bolts chased the Valerian Coop Infiltrator into the sky.

"What about pursuit?" Naomi asked. "Is the *Albright* lifting?"

Rudy's squat head spun, turning his large optical sensor toward Naomi. "Baxter and I ensured the *Albright* will not be lifting off anytime soon."

The *Osprey* roared, gaining more and more altitude. Jax had the main thrusters near full power. No space control or Imperial assholes to yell at him, so why not? Plus, he had a fight in orbit to get to. If he was being honest, he was a little excited at the prospect of slagging some unruly spacers.

"Looks like three freighters. One might have some teeth, the other two look like they're held together with glue," Naomi reported. "Wait. Wow. Okay, I take back what I just said. Sorta."

"Sorta?" Jax repeated.

The tactical screen at Jax's right updated with the locations all three ships. He flipped a few switches. "Weapons hot. Particle beam is charging."

"Shields are up," Skip added.

Jax noticed the better armed ship first but then saw what had caused Naomi to change her assessment. The second ship, an old freighter that someone went to great lengths to make look like a piece of crap, was, in fact, almost as well armed as the lead ship. He whistled.

"We're being hailed," Skip informed.

A small screen to Jax's left blinked to life, showing a rather bedraggled woman. She was in more or less typical spacer coveralls, oil stains and all. "We just want the data. Abano says you stole it."

"'Stole' is such a harsh word," Jax said.

"We're being targeted," Naomi said.

The woman on the screen said, "This doesn't have to get ugly."

One of the freighters, the one least armed of the trio, was moving to block the *Osprey*'s path. Jax pressed a few buttons, and his targeting screen showed a bright red bracket around the offending ship.

"One warning," Jax said. The woman on screen frowned. "Come on, kid. Whatever it is you stole from Marcus, just hand it over, and we'll let you go. You can go back to whatever pissant jobs you normally do. You're outnumbered and out-gunned."

Jax tilted his head. "I won't try to sugarcoat this. Your pal talked too loud, and now you all are gonna lose your score." He pressed the trigger on his flight stick, and the brilliant purple beam of the *Osprey*'s only real weapon leaped between the two ships. The freighter's meager shields, meant to keep micro meteors and the occasional pirate blaster at bay while the ship made an escape, collapsed immediately.

The particle beam punched through the ship's hull like it was nothing more than tissue paper. Jax had made sure to target the cargo hold, hoping the crew followed best practice on ships like that, keeping the hold secured and sealed.

Atmosphere and a few mismatched cargo crates vented from the matching holes on the side of the ship.

The woman on the comm screen shouted, "What the hell is wrong with you?" He noticed that her image had not wavered. She was on one of the other ships.

Jax looked at her, shrugging. "Like I said. There's only one way this—"

"Missile's inbound," Naomi interrupted.

Jax slapped the button that closed the comm channel, pulling his flight stick as far to the right as he could, while pushing the throttle control forward. The *Osprey* tilted. The planet below vanished from view.

"Five, no, six contacts. Time to impact, twenty seconds," Skip said, his voice calmer than either human occupant of the bridge.

"Jax..." Naomi said.

Jax consulted his tactical display. The stricken freighter was no longer a red icon but a pale pink.

The incoming missiles, however, were very red. Bright red. Imminent death red. The freighter that fired them was equally red, the one that had been masked to look less lethal than it was.

The *Osprey* banked, then inverted and swooped in a tight arc, presenting her top side, the side that had the small infiltrator's missile launchers. Six small hatches popped open along the ship's spine.

"Firing," Jax said as the sound of the top mounted launcher's cycling echoed. Small hunter-killer missiles leaped from the ship, their targeting computers locked onto the incoming missiles. A second *ca-thunk* sound, and another round of hunter killers took flight.

"Set up the next round for ship killers," Jax said to no one in particular, assuming Naomi or Skip would handle it.

Energy bolts struck the *Osprey*'s shields, lighting them up. The more heavily armed freighter had powered up and was trying the same maneuver its friend had tried and failed to execute. Jax liked its odds more than the previous ship's.

"If you can get us here," Rudy said, sending a nav plot to Jax's station, "we can open a wormhole and get the hell out of here."

Jax's screen updated with a flight path. He'd have to get around the larger, armed freighter.

"Missiles neutralized," Skip announced. The ship rocked several times as more blaster fire raked the shields, opaquing them in places.

"Maybe try to not kill them?" Naomi said.

Jax pulled the flight control all the way toward him. The *Osprey* roared through another maneuver, bulkheads groaning. Jax looked over his shoulder. "Why exactly would I do that? They're not exactly pulling punches."

"Because there's no need. Do you really want to be known as the guy that just kills people willy-nilly?" Naomi said, her expression flat.

Jax sighed. "Set the missiles in the rack to concussion. Fire when we're in range."

"Copy," Skip said.

"You're almost there," Rudy said, trying to sound encouraging. The ship shook.

The telltale clunks of the dorsal missile tubes cycling their deadly payloads echoed through the ship, followed by the sound of six launches. "Missiles away," Skip announced.

Through the transparent titanium viewscreen, Jax could see the lead freighter banking hard to reverse its course and get some distance from the oncoming missiles. The only slightly less armed freighter did its best to intercept the incoming missiles, even succeeding a few times. Those missiles that got through— that normally would have battered down the ship's meager shields, then ripped its hull apart—did neither of those things. Set for concussion, the missiles impacted the shields, delivering staggering blows that would overload shield emitters but cause no lasting damage to the ship.

The *Osprey* slipped past the much larger vessel. As the two ships passed, Jax looked out the transparent viewscreen and waved. Given the distance between the *Osprey* and the other ship, he wasn't sure if the gesture he received back was a wave or something more off-color.

The navigation display updated to show a clear flight line out of the system. "You're clear for wormhole," Rudy announced.

Jax checked the power readings on the small diagnostic screen that monitored the wormhole generator. Everything was in the green. Thankfully, the firefight had spared the delicate piece of equipment. He activated the generator and watched as a purple and green smudge appeared about a hundred thousand kilometers ahead. Within seconds, as the distance closed, the smudge became the familiar swirling space-bruise of an open wormhole. The *Osprey* dove into the rip in space-time, the hole closing behind it.

Outside the clear viewscreens that surrounded most of the bridge, the swirling colors of the wormhole played across faces and control panels. "I could use a shower," Jax said, putting the flight controls into standby, giving full control of the ship over to Skip.

"Yes, you could," Naomi agreed, eyebrow arched.

He smirked. "How about you all get started decrypting Abano's latest clue?" He left the bridge.

Captain Marcus Abano threw a can of beer across the hold. "Fuck!" he screamed for what might have been the one hundredth time since the infuriating scout ship had taken off.

The crew he had left in orbit had reported their complete failure at stopping the thieves.

The two Delphino brothers looked at each other, then their captor and maybe business partners. Steve finally raised his hand, slowly. "So, you don't know where to go?"

Abano turned, his face a mask of fury. "No! Like I told you. I didn't trust myself, or the people I tend to run with, just having the coordinates to a fucking fortune's worth of salvage. I hired task workers to take each piece, log it and hide it. That way none of them knew what they were doing or the next part in the chain." He took a deep breath, kicked a piece of equipment. "Foolproof," he whispered. He slapped his palms on his thighs and stomped up the stairs into the ship's crew spaces.

The Delphinos looked at each other and the two surviving spacers from the other ship Abano had brought in on the score. Everyone shrugged.

Marshall said, "Well, this is super fucked up. I'm gonna

strangle Jax, maybe Naomi, too." His brother, normally the cooler headed of the two, nodded his agreement.

One of the other men in the hold stood and walked toward the stairs up into the main section of the ship. "I'll make sure he's getting us underway." He looked at the two brothers. "You can come aboard the *Legendary*. We'll take you back to Del Rio Two." The Delphinos nodded. The other man followed his crew mate.

Steve looked at his brother. "I can't believe Jax screwed us like that."

His brother clucked. "I can. That little weasel." He sighed. "But we'd have done the same to him, so..."

Hitching a thumb toward the general direction of the *Albright*'s bridge, Steve said, "I can't believe that idiot was so paranoid that he hired people to hide these clues without leaving himself some sort of backdoor, failsafe."

Marshall nodded, holding up a fist for his brother to bump.

Rudy rolled into engineering to find Baxter in his charging dock. *Are you online?* he sent. He placed the encrypted data storage unit they stole from Abano's hiding place on Cornucopia on the workstation.

More or less, Baxter answered. *I believe I've isolated the problem.*

That's good news, Rudy replied.

Only sort of. That energy round I took fried my secondary sub-processor management suite and hardware assembly.

Rudy rolled further into the space, toward his friend's recharging cradle. The space was empty and well maintained. Jax only went into engineering when he had to and couldn't find an alternative. Baxter kept it clean, and Skip handled directing the other droids in repairs. It worked. Rudy turned his large optic sensor to his friend. *Can you make repairs?*

No. I need a new module.

That's bad. They don't make those any more. Your railgun assemblies were incredibly difficult to acquire. I don't recall seeing secondary sub-processor hardware even listed.

It is. I've been trying to manage the sub-processes myself, but

I'm burning out processors. Baxter stepped from his docking station. He pointed to a bin next to the industrial fabricator. *I've been able to stay ahead of it, but it is getting more difficult and the cores are burning out faster and faster.*

Rudy rolled over to the bin. His optic sensor took in the pile of processing cores. He turned to Baxter. "This seems bad," he said aloud.

From the ceiling, Skip said, "It is. The fabricator cannot keep up with Baxter's demand. Processing cores burn out print heads fast. Really fast."

Rudy's squat, cylindrical head spun. "Okay, then what do we do?"

"I make peace with my end," Baxter said, his optic sensor swishing back and forth, a sinister red. "I've reached the end of my useful life."

Rudy was silent, his own processors running through simulated options as rapidly as possible. Finally, he said, "Unacceptable. I will consult with Jax and Naomi."

"No," Baxter said. He moved to his small friend. "I am Jackson's protector. I will do that until I cannot. That is—was—my function."

The ship shuddered.

"What was that?" Rudy asked.

"Don't get overwrought," Baxter said to the ceiling.

Switching back to the private wireless network the ship and droids shared, *Power surge,* Skip answered. *Don't flatter yourself.*

The hatch opened ahead of Rudy zipping out of engineering. As he rolled through the mostly empty cargo hold, his head turned to look back toward engineering. *Take it easy, Baxter. Please.*

Jax had just stepped out of the common head in the forward section of the ship. "What the hell happened?" He looked around. He spotted Rudy zipping past on his way up to the bridge.

"Power surge in the backup power bus," Skip replied.

"Serious?" Jax continued toward the aft section of the common deck, where the crew berths were, including his own.

"Serious enough. I've taken us out of the wormhole. We're in deep space. I'm reviewing telemetry now, but the likely cause is damage caused by a blaster shot that got through our shields."

Jax opened the hatch to his quarters. Rudy's neat freak tendencies annoyed Naomi to no end, but Jax had learned long ago to lean into them. He walked to his dresser, opening his t-shirt drawer to find two rows of neatly folded shirts organized by color. He selected a bright blue shirt with a retro Galactic Rangers logo on the front.

"Something Baxter can take care of?" he asked as he grabbed a pair of gray, multi-pocketed work pants.

There was a noticeable pause before Skip answered, "No, this is probably something you should take care of."

Jax slipped his boots on and stood up. "Okay, sure." The hatch opened, and he ran into Naomi. "Jib jab!" He stumbled backward.

"Jib jab?" she repeated, hand on her hip.

"What're you doing creepin' around?" Jax regained his composure and pushed past her. "I need to suit up."

"Skip was just filling me in. You need any help?" She fell in behind him as he entered the common area.

"Yeah. You can monitor things from the equipment bay, in case we need to disconnect anything from the inside."

She nodded. "Sounds good."

While Jax suited up, Naomi made her way up to the cramped mechanical space above the crew quarters. It was the same level as the bridge, but only accessible via a ladder in the corridor outside the berths. It was a cramped space, barely enough clearance for her to stand, and only really in the center of the oblong space.

Several key pieces of shipboard equipment were either housed in the cramped work space or connected to it.

Conduits, wires, and pipes filled the walls, and machinery lined the floor and ceiling. The ceiling equipment was meant to be repairable from the inside of the ship, as well as from outside. The alluvial damper that Jax and Jeffry had repaired on their recent trip to New Terra was situated just aft of the equipment bay. As far as Naomi was concerned, a design flaw for sure.

She tapped her earpiece. "I'm in the equipment bay."

"Copy that," Jax said. His voice had an odd pitch to it; he was fully suited up and had his helmet on and sealed. "I'll be there in a minute."

While she waited, she looked around. This was actually the first time she'd been up there. As expected for a ship Jax operated, there were few labels and numerous clear signs of fast, often jury-rigged, repairs: duct tape here, something zip-tied to another thing over there. Something with a slow drip leak leaving an evaporating pool on the deck. She sighed.

Overhead, she heard the heavy footsteps of space suited, magnetized feet. Jax said, "Okay, I'm here. I see the damage. Glad I brought the duct tape." Naomi rubbed her face.

CHAPTER 9

The Valerian Coop designed the Infiltrator Model Five to be a workhorse. Fast, stealthy, and maneuverable, they served private citizens, shipping companies, and the militaries of the Independent Systems Alliance for decades before becoming the fast attack craft of the Indies against the Separatists. Meant to be easily repairable in situ, they served well, and while less common anymore, used to be one of the more commonly seen ships in orbit over colonies or patrolling space stations.

The Coop went under after the war, rather than be taken over by the Empire. Ever since, infiltrators and their larger cousins, the Mark Nine Sloop had become harder and harder to come by.

The damage caused by the blaster bolt was minor. A lucky shot, to be sure. It had penetrated the shields and hit a piece of hull plating that was improperly grounded. Likely Jax's fault, not that he'd admit that to Naomi or the droids. The burned duct tape was a dead giveaway. Once he had the panel off, the fix was easy. More duct tape. He secured the wire that likely caused the problem to the side of the space so it wouldn't stray.

After slapping some duct tape over the wire, he pushed the panel back into place.

To be safe, he had asked Naomi to disconnect a few things from inside the small equipment bay, almost right underneath him. "Okay, Naomi. Reconnect the secondary bus. Then flip the breaker back." He paused. "Wait—no. Sorry."

"Wait? Sorry?"

"Reverse that. Make sure the breaker is engaged. Otherwise, you might fry yourself."

"You're sure?" Her voice made it clear that she wasn't interested in dying right then.

"Yes. I think."

"I hate you. Here goes." In the background there was a loud clack as she pushed the breaker closed.

A second later, a small panel next to the wiring bundle Jax was working on came to life. Two LEDs flashed red, then settled on green. "Good job." He closed up the compartment.

Self-sealing hull panels were a wonder. No bolts to worry about losing, just matching memory metal components that, when put together and supplied a mild current, formed a super strong bond.

Just as the panel locked in place, something knocked Jax off of his feet—or would have, if they were not magnetically attached to the hull. As it was, he tipped sideways, barely able to angle himself so that he didn't do any damage to his knees. His back, or rather the EVA suit's backpack, hit the hull, hard.

"Shit!" he hissed.

"What's wrong?" Naomi demanded. When he didn't answer, she said, "Jax?"

"What is wrong?" Skip asked on the shared comm channel. "Oh, I see. There is an alert on your suit. Captain, you are losing pressure. Your vitals are all over the place."

"Oh, am I?" Jax huffed. "So I am. I guess I could use some

help out here." The last few words slurred into one jumble of syllables.

Through the comm line, Naomi could hear air hissing out of this suit. His voice was muffled. He said, "Micro...meteor. Through my...leg. Losing...air, and...blood."

She crouch-walked to the opening in the deck and the ladder back down to the common deck. "I'll suit up."

"No time," Skip said. He switched to the droids' wireless network. *Baxter, Jackson needs you.*

I'm on my way, the combat droid replied, already heading down the stairs to the boarding room. The moment his head cleared the threshold between cargo deck and boarding room, the airlock seal slid closed, sealing off the boarding room from the rest of the ship. The ramp deployed, stopping short to form a platform parallel to the deck to walk out onto. Several internal diagnostic alarms went off inside Baxter's main processing stack. Two more sub-processors were on the verge of collapse. He redistributed processing to his weapons systems since he wouldn't need weapons to save Jackson. The alarms went silent.

Baxter disengaged the magnetic locks built into his feet and magnetized his hands, planting them on the hull and levering himself up and around to latch his feet onto the hull.

He strode up and over the side of the ship and spied Jax, his feet stuck to the hull, his body drifting, arms up forming a T. His left leg was a bloody mess, the damage sufficient that the self-sealing capabilities of the suit weren't able to make repairs. Baxter's sensors immediately pinpointed the half-inch hole in the leg of the space suit, flash frozen blood around the hole. A pair of matching plumes of escaping air were visible. The micro meteor had gone straight through Jax's leg. The frozen blood had formed an imperfect seal.

He walked as fast as he could over to Jax. He wirelessly

deactivated his captain's mag boots, clutching him as he hustled back down toward the boarding room.

I have him.

Naomi ran through the cargo hold to the small med bay. The auto-doc came alive. The monitor at the head of the bio-bed read, *Provide patient.*

"Calm down, he's coming," Naomi said.

She leaned out of the small space to see Baxter come up the stairs, Jax's limp space-suited body cradled in his arms. She ran over to intercept and followed Baxter, stripping off Jax's space suit as the pair moved toward the med bay. By the time they reached the bio-bed, most of the suit had been removed. Blood caked his insulating undergarment.

The bio-bed monitor immediately began displaying Jax's vital signs. The spiderlike unit lowered and began cutting his pants apart to get to the wound. Naomi stood to the side, transfixed by the blood. Baxter took a step towards the med bay door and stopped.

Naomi turned. "You okay?" No reply. "Baxter?" She put a hand on his shoulder. He didn't move.

Behind her, the auto-doc was busy with Jackson.

"Skip, what's wrong with Baxter?" Naomi asked, looking up at the ceiling. She pushed on the inert bot. He didn't budge.

After a pause, the ship's SI replied, "What do you mean?"

Naomi looked from the ceiling to the inert combat droid in front of her. Behind her, the auto-doc was busily beeping to itself as it ministered to Jax. "What do you mean, what do I mean? He's standing here, doing...well, nothing." She waved a hand in front of the big bot's optic sensor.

"Uh..."

"Out with it," Naomi snapped, turning to the nearest camera.

Rudy appeared, rolling over to the inert combat droid. "Great."

Naomi glared at the small droid. "What are you three up to?"

Rudy rolled over so that he could lean past Naomi to look into the med bay. He straightened back up and rolled toward the center of the cargo hold. He waved Naomi over. She wiggled past Baxter, who had frozen in the doorway of the med bay. When she reached him, he said, "Baxter is damaged."

Naomi looked over her shoulder. "Can't his self-repair systems, or his charging cradle, take care of it?" Rudy pointed at Baxter, still motionless. She grunted. "Okay. Obviously not. So, what're we doing about it? Why didn't you guys tell us?"

Rudy fidgeted. "Baxter insisted we not tell Jackson, and by extension, you."

"Why?"

Skip answered. "Baxter is a combat droid. A model that hasn't been in production in eighteen years. Parts are hard to come by. He wanted to die with dignity. Protecting Jackson."

"Die? How serious is it?" Naomi rubbed her hands together, looking at the big droid. She frowned, then exhaled, slapping her hands on her thighs. "Great, droids with honor codes." Turning to Rudy. "New topic. How's the decryption coming?"

"Slowly."

"Stay on it." She turned and walked back to Baxter. She inhaled and put both hands on his matte black chest, her bio-circuitry tattoos lighting up.

Baxter?

Naomi? What are you doing? I did not know you could do this.

Me either. I was going to ask you that. You just gonna make him wake up one morning and you aren't there?

I could leave a note.

Don't be a smart ass. How can I help?

You can't.

Don't be so defeatist.

Rudy watched for a second or two while Naomi and Baxter communed, then rolled back to engineering where Skip was working on the data storage module. The storage unit was on the workbench, connected to the main processing core. The main engineering display was showing the estimated progress on the decryption. The progress bar was sluggishly creeping across the screen.

This is taking forever, Rudy beamed.

Sorry, I'm not a code breaker, Skip quipped. *Wait, since we're just sitting here, I can pull additional resources from wormhole navigation.*

Rudy's head spun. *Will that be enough?*

Maybe. It'll be more than we have at the moment.

The progress bar jumped closer to the far side of the display. Rudy bobbed on his smart material ball. *Okay, then.*

The auto-doc had cut away Jax's trousers. Half of its spider-like limbs were working on the entry and exit wound, while the rest were working on the frozen flesh around the wounds. To make its work easier, it was keeping Jax fully sedated.

Twenty-odd years ago, a young Jackson Caruso was playing on the floor of the Caruso family mechanical bay with Baxter. The matte black droid was holding two model starships, waving them toward the model young Jackson was playing with.

His parents had taken Rudy and the *Osprey* out a few days prior. He didn't understand what they did when they left, but when they left, Baxter and his Memaw took care of him.

The hatch that led in to the station slid open, allowing Lucy Caruso and Assistant Trade Minister Neeti Singh to enter the mechanical bay. Baxter turned. "Ms. Caruso. Assistant Trade Minister." His angry red scatter light optical sensor swished back and forth.

The elder Caruso smiled, leaving the trade minister to stand near the hatch. "Hello, Baxter." She looked at Jax, still playing with his model spaceship. "Jackson dear, come here."

The little boy stood and handed his spaceship to Baxter.

The droid's optic sensor followed the boy as he met his grand-mother. He walked over to his Memaw, who was kneeling.

Lucy looked past the boy to the combat droid and shook her head once. She looked at Jax. "Jackson, I need to tell you some-thing about your mommy and daddy."

The station-wide public address system came to life. "Atten-tion, please. Imperial vessels arriving. All citizens please wait for further information."

Baxter dropped the toy spaceships.

Jax's eyes twitched under his eyelids. As his mind came back to the present, the sense of dull aching pain came with it. Something made a series of happy-sounding beeps. A voice, further away than the happy beeping thing, said, "He's coming to."

Jax opened his eyes just a little. It was so bright out. "What happened?"

"You almost died." Whose voice was that?

"He did not. Stop being melodramatic." Was that a woman's voice?

"His heart did stop once." The first voice. Rudy?

Jax opened his eyes. "Rudy?" He looked around. He was in the med bay on the *Osprey*. How had he gotten there? Was he naked?

"Well, he's better now, so let's get a move on. Who knows if Abano and his friends were able to piece together any clues or anything about the next stop?" Naomi looked down at Jax. "Glad you're not dead."

"Me, too," he croaked. He remembered now. He had been on the outer hull making a repair. A micro meteor had punctured his suit, and him. They had been on their way somewhere. Where?

Rudy tapped on the side of the bed. "We decrypted the data module. We're ready to head to the next stop on this little scavenger hunt."

Jax looked over at him, his brain still a bit fuzzy. The droid's rust-colored head was barely visible next to the bio-bed. "That's good. Where are we going?"

"Tycho," the nav droid replied.

That wiped away a large percentage of Jax's brain fog. Tycho station, one of the first independently owned and operated space stations to fall to the Empire. The Unification War hadn't even officially been declared when the Unity Militia, as they called themselves, appeared and surrounded the station.

Tycho station was older than most other stations, founded in the early days of humanity's expansion. Tycho Shipping Solutions wanted a base of operations in the expansion sectors and decided to relocate their corporate offices to show their support for the early colonies. It had also been wildly profitable to be nearer the new shipping routes.

The decades of expansion and their early locking down of market share in the region saw Tycho Shipping Solutions' profits soar and Tycho station's size quadruple.

The earlier images of the station show it looking somewhat similar to Kelso station. Now, however, you'd never see the resemblance. The central docking structure became a hub for four two-kilometer-long spokes, each a few hundred meters in diameter. After they completed the spokes, a new, much more massive, ring had been constructed, making the station temporarily look like a space station from old Earth vids, minus the spin.

The outer ring was almost entirely space dock facilities, commercial areas, low rent residential, and less legal things.

Eventually, the next phase of expansion began, transforming the outer ring, adding large docking towers that ran vertically at ninety degrees to the ring. The towers added more storage and docking capacity, further cementing Tycho's grip on trade and transport in that sector and several neighbors.

Jax sat up, stopping along the way to let the spinning in his head subside. "Skip, you have the route plotted?"

"Sure do, Captain," the ceiling replied.

Once he was sure he could do it, Jax spun his legs off the bio-bed, planting his feet on the deck. He grabbed the thin sheet that was covering him, keeping it in place.

"Careful," Rudy advised, rolling backward in case Jax fell. Naomi just watched.

His left leg ached like crazy, but otherwise, seemed to be able to bear his weight. The auto-doc had wrapped a white bandage around his leg above the knee. He took a step, then another. "I think I—" He collapsed, hitting the deck as Rudy darted out of the way. He looked over at his metal friend, then up at Naomi, who had moved closer, scowling. "Thanks."

"You're heavy," the droid offered by way of excuse. He rolled over and pulled the sheet back over Jax. Without another word, the rust-colored nav droid left the med bay.

Naomi shrugged. "He's not wrong."

Jax hadn't been thrilled to find out two full days had passed since what he called the "too many holes in Jax" incident. Rudy and Skip explained that it couldn't be avoided. They didn't know where to go, and going somewhere at random would have not only consumed the processing power they needed to get done sooner but could have potentially—almost certainly, in fact —had them heading in the wrong direction.

That it had taken almost that long to decrypt the data drive helped smooth over his annoyance, as well.

Jax looked over the navigation data. "Fine, you're right." He checked the power readings on the wormhole generator and pushed the *Osprey* up to speed before opening the tear in space-time. As the flight controls folded back into the console, he said, "I could really go for nachos."

Naomi, sitting at her console playing a video about cats that trailed rainbows, looked up. "I could do nachos."

One of Jax's standing rules was that whenever they docked or landed, Rudy was to stock up the pantry.

Years ago, making what, at the time, should have been a simple run to New Cairo, the wormhole drive had failed. The

Osprey fell out of her wormhole in deep space. Luckily, the comm system was unaffected, but help was several days away. Someone could have gotten there sooner, but it would have cost more. Jax opted for economy saving over premium grade.

What he had not known was that the ship's stores were almost empty. The plan had been to restock on New Cairo. Their drop off was in Baltim, and he had heard there was an amazing koshari place near the spaceport and some good shopping in the market nearby.

By the time the rescue ship arrived, Jax was licking ration bar wrappers and watering down one last bulb of soda. Ever since, most anything Jax could think up on the fly could be made, so long as it was mostly unhealthy crap.

"Steak or chicken?" he asked, opening the refrigerator.

"Steak," Naomi said. She moved to the pantry and started rummaging around. "We have a new spice packet I picked up. We can try that on the meat."

Jax grunted his agreement and began preparing the rest of the needed ingredients.

While the steak sizzled on the cooktop, Jax looked around. "Where's Baxter?"

Rudy, charging in his cradle next to the large entertainment display, turned his head, optic sensor spinning. Jax looked at him, and he turned his sensor away.

Jax turned to Naomi, who had moved on to grating cheese. She whispered, "Coward," under her breath. She turned to Jax. "You might want to sit down."

He turned on her. "What? What's wrong?" He looked up. "Skip, where's Baxter?"

"Captain, he's in engineering. You should—" Jax bolted for the staircase. "Let Naomi explain," the SI finished.

Naomi watched him disappear down the stairs. Biting her

lip, she went to the cooktop and continued cooking the seasoned steak.

Jax burst into engineering, the hatch already open for him, thanks to Skip. "Baxter!" He looked around. The matte black combat droid was in his charging station. He walked over. "You okay, buddy?"

The red scatter light of Baxter's optical sensor array came to life. "No." Before Jax could say anything, he continued, "I was damaged when we robbed Abano. There is nothing we can do. Parts are simply no longer available." He put a heavy metal hand on Jax's shoulder. "We've had a long run, Jackson. It has been my pleasure to see you grow up. To protect you."

Jax's eyes glistened, tears ready to emerge. He started to say something, and his voice caught in this throat. He looked down, then tried again. "Bax, buddy. We'll figure this out. You're not done." He snuffled, a gross wet noise. Baxter leaned back. "I'm not done with you," Jax said, still looking down.

The tall droid inclined his head. "We don't always get a choice." He leaned down and wrapped Jax in a hug, careful to manage the pressure he was applying so as to not pop his human friend like a grape.

PART THREE

CHAPTER 10

When the Unification War broke out, the Unity Militia came knocking on Tycho station's door. The rumor was that they were already en route before the first shots had been recorded. When the fleet showed up, it caught Tycho's managers flat footed. Worse yet, the local Alliance forces were equally unprepared.

The Militia fleet decimated the minimal Alliance presence before sending a single word to Tycho, "Surrender."

The terms were simple and, to the surprise of Tycho's executives, not wholly unfavorable. They remained in control of the station and their company. They simply worked for the soon-to-be new order now.

"I've updated the transponder," Naomi said from the ceiling speaker. She was in the technical crawl space again, this time with the access panel to the transceiver array open. The ability to swap identities was not factor standard on Valerian Coop Infiltrators. It was, in fact, illegal, even before the Empire. The *Osprey* was special in that regard. A gift from Jax's parents.

Jax was sitting at his pilot's station. He looked at a small display and nodded. "Looks good. We're squawking as the..." He groaned. "The *Parakeet*. Really?"

"You said, pick a bird. Besides, I like parakeets," Naomi defended, closing up the panel and making her way to the opening in the floor. She sidestepped a puddle of who knew what. "Jax," she hissed.

The *Osprey* was about to drop out of her wormhole. The moment she did, the space control system of Tycho would lock on and query her identity. The *Parakeet* was registered out of New Egypt as a courier.

Jax had done just enough work under that ident to keep it up to date. "Real space in ten," he announced.

The moment the counter hit zero, he eased the power lever for the wormhole generator back. Naomi was coming up the stairs as the vortex of non-relative space stretched and distorted until a fissure appeared, stars visible beyond it.

"Damn," Naomi whispered. "I knew it was big, but..."

"That's what he —" Jax started.

"No," Naomi interrupted. She pointed. "Are there normally so many Imperial heavies hanging around?" Outside the transparent titanium viewscreen, three Adjudicator class warships were lazily orbiting the station, several hundred kilometers distant.

Jax looked up through the transparent viewscreen. "Yeah. I mean, I've only been here twice, but both times there was a... presence." One of the ships, the *Hammer*, drifted past.

"Incoming comms," Skip announced.

The monitor near the ceiling blinked to life. A stern-faced Imperial ensign appeared. She cleared her throat. "Independent courier *Parakeet*, please prepare for auto flight take over." Her bored expression made it clear she didn't care what his answer was. She knew as well as Jax did that if he declined, the nearby *Hammer* would chase him off or destroy him.

"Tycho station, confirmed. We're ready for auto flight," Jax replied. A second later, an icon appeared on his console. He tapped it and the flight controls retracted into the console.

"Welcome to Tycho station...*Parakeet.*" The screen went black a moment too late to hide the woman's smirk.

"She was laughing at us," Jax groused.

"Probably. So?" Naomi replied.

Ahead of them, Tycho station was growing in size. They were on course for one of the docking towers that rose from the ring.

The upside of Tycho station being as big as it was: there were plenty of docking facilities for ships of all sizes among the various towers. The tower that the *Osprey* was approaching could easily hold a half dozen ships her size. The entire top of the tower was an open flight deck. The glow of a static atmosphere barrier was visible.

The *Osprey* passed through the barrier and rotated to face out. Her landing gear extended with a series of *thunks*. One more *thunk* and a slight tilting of the deck, and the ship was down.

"Welcome to Tycho station," Jax said, his voice flat. He looked at Naomi and Rudy. "What now?"

Naomi looked out the viewports, watching Tycho station staff and ship crews bustle about the flight deck outside. "I need access to the station's computer. The storage module had two pieces of data in it: the coordinates for Tycho, and a string of numbers." Jax made a *go on* motion. She continued, "Rudy, Skip, and I ran the numbers through everything we could think of. Zilch. I'm guessing they're significant to the station."

Jax hunched his shoulders. "Okay. So, what? We just go out and find a terminal?"

"If only," Naomi replied.

Rudy added, "Unfortunately, I can't leave the ship, and

well, Skip is the ship. We'll need way more processing power than," he hitched a metal thumb toward Naomi, "she's got, no offense."

"None taken." Naomi smiled.

Skip added, "You need to hook me up to a data trunk line. Rudy and I can hijack the station's computer and crunch the numbers to figure out what this last clue is."

Jax followed Naomi down the stairs, Rudy passing them in his null gravity tube in the center of the spiral staircase. Jax reached the sofa and collapsed onto it. "A data trunk line? They don't just leave those lying around." He sat up and looked at Naomi. "Right?"

She tossed him a beer and said, "Not likely, no." She sat on the chair next to the sofa. "We'll have to find one and pull it up or tap it." She took a long pull of her drink, and after sighing, added, "Upside, it's not like they guard the data trunk lines. They just don't leave them publicly accessible. So, as long as we can manage to not attract attention, we're good."

The *Osprey*'s boarding ramp unfolded as it lowered. Unlike at Kelso station, there was no customs agent waiting to interview the crew and check the ship's flight logs and transponder against filed flight plans.

Jax and Naomi stepped off the ramp. The circular landing facility was a hive of activity. Imperial dock workers moved about like bees in a flower garden.

A customs inspection would still happen if someone tried to leave the space dock level to enter the station proper. Tycho station often served as a way station and transfer point. Ships arrived, offloaded, and departed the station without ever disembarking crew. Dock workers in power load lifters stomped between ships and cargo lifts moving goods here and there. The station opted to not hassle people until they wanted to actually enter the station.

Jax looked around. He rubbed his left leg, even though it didn't hurt at as much as it did before. "Over there." He pointed toward the center of the circular space and the massive hub supporting the top of the docking bay and its several levels of offices and storage areas. The hub contained cargo lifts, dock worker facilities, short term storage, and other administrative stuff that Jax never cared to learn about.

They walked across the deck toward the hub and the hatch marked *Station Personnel Only* that Jax hoped was a locker room.

The hatch slid open when Jax pressed the access panel. Naomi looked around. "This feels familiar."

He shrugged and held out his arm. "Maybe we can find work in cosplay?"

"As janitors? No, thanks," Naomi said, walking past him.

The locker room was empty. It didn't take long to find two dock team uniforms—clean ones, even. They walked back onto the space dock. Jax tapped his earpiece. "Okay, Skip. Where to?" Around them, similarly dressed men and women came and went, never looking at the two workers once.

Rudy was in engineering, working on the fabricator set in the corner. The device was busily assembling a specially designed data cable with a specially designed, self-sealing tap on the end. Once Jax and Naomi tapped into the data trunk, Rudy would plug the other end into the primary IO port in the main processing core. Rudy turned his large optical sensor toward his friend. Over the shared wireless network, he beamed, *Baxter*.

Yes?

How are you doing?

My systems are operating at the minimal possible levels to keep me online. I can't leave my docking cradle because my few remaining sub-processors will overheat and melt down. How are you?

Skip interrupted, *Stay on target.*

Over the shared comms, Skip replied to Jax, "I'm picking up thickly shielded cabling near that ugly freighter with the old Earth Dutch flag garishly painted on the side. Honestly, no style."

Jax and Naomi looked around. The latter pointed, saying, "The tap ready?"

"Yes," Rudy replied.

"I'll grab it," Naomi said, heading back toward the *Osprey*. She ducked as a power load lifter swung a three-meter square cargo module overhead.

Jax looked around again. The Dutch-flagged freighter was a newer model Daimler-Benz Mega Lift XJ-830. The crew was either aboard the vessel or somewhere in the station. From all appearances, the ground crew had already finished its work and moved on. The ship was powered down, and no one was around.

Jax spotted a section of deck plating that had yellow and black striped tape around the edges. "Found an access panel."

Naomi appeared, unspooling a thick cable behind her as she walked from the *Osprey*. "Won't someone notice this?"

Skip answered, "If you can hurry up, I'll log a record in the station's records to explain it."

Jax moved to help carry the thick cable. "Plus, as long as we look like we have a purpose, no one will bother us."

They reached the panel, and Jax popped that latch. The access space was full of cables and conduits. Jax looked up at Naomi. "Any idea which one?"

She looked down into the hole in the deck, then up at Jax. "Not really."

"It'll be yellow," Skip offered. "Probably."

Jax made a face and shrugged. He pointed to the yellow data cable tucked in among dozens of other randomly colored cables. It was as thick as his arm. He reached in and tugged on the cable, pushing others away from it.

Naomi reached in, clamping the homemade tap around the wire. The device made a noise as she secured it. A small plume of bluish smoke wafted up, the smell of burned insulation following it. She recoiled and brushed the smoke away.

Jax peered over his shoulder at the *Osprey*. "That work?"

"Wait one," Skip replied.

Aboard the *Osprey*, Rudy was in his cradle on the bridge. *Scanning the data coming over the tap.* He beamed to Skip, *This place has an RI. Will you be able to keep it busy?*

After a few milliseconds' pause, the ship's SI replied, *I'll have to. If it reports our presence, the Imperials will be on us instantly. I'll need your help.*

Rudy's head made a slow circle. *Of course.*

Skip answered Jax. "Yes, that is it. We're set here, Captain. You and Naomi should go into the station, explore. This will take some time."

Naomi eased the hatch back down, resting it on the data cable. "Skip, can you set up some credentials for us?"

A few seconds passed. "Done."

"Welcome to Tycho station," the bored-looking Imperial customs agent said. She smiled at Jax, then Naomi. "Family reunion, huh?"

Jax coughed. He tilted his head towards Naomi. "Adopted."

The customs agent blinked and moved her glossy-eyed gaze from Jax to Naomi and back. "Uh huh." She pointed toward the hatch and the transit lobby beyond. "Have fun."

"Your ship has a weird sense of humor," Naomi said as they rode the transit car, first down to the ring, then laterally to the nearest spoke, then in toward the central hub.

Jax grunted. "Tell me about it."

The car slowed, then stopped. The doors parted.

The central hub of Tycho station looked like a shopping mall scaled up a thousandfold. The administrative facilities had long been moved to the ring, along with most of the residential sections. The hub was over a hundred tiered decks with shopping, dining, entertainment, and more.

Jax turned to Naomi. "So, food?"

She nodded, looking around. "Hey, do you think there's a—"

Jax held up a hand. "We are not eating at TGIFriday's."

"Killjoy."

In the center of the hollow entertainment complex, mechanical art constructs floated on repulsor lifts, performing an intricate ballet. Segmented constructs twisted and turned, metal ouroboros symbols inverting on each other.

Jax pointed directly across and three levels up. "Chinese?" Spinning holographic text read Wuhan Palace in a half-dozen languages. Naomi smiled.

Wuhan Palace did not disappoint. Jax looked at the spread arrayed between him and Naomi. "We might have over-ordered."

"Don't wuss out on me, Caruso," Naomi said, stabbing a dumpling with one of her chopsticks. She popped the morsel in her mouth, and around chews, said, "So, Baxter."

Jax plucked a piece of kung pao chicken from the platter in front of him. He chewed slowly, composing his thoughts. This place really did make a mean kung pao. He met Naomi's gaze and said, "Yeah." He took a breath and let it out. "I don't know what I'll do if he dies."

Naomi helped herself to some Yushan eggplant. "We'll figure something out." She winked. "Tell me about him."

Jax took another bite, thinking back to when he first met Baxter. "I was just a kid when my mom and dad introduced me to Baxter."

Back aboard the *Osprey*, Rudy and Skip were sifting through Tycho station's computer for clues of any kind as to what Abano's mysterious number meant.

The station's Rudimentary Intelligence had proven to be no serious threat. Tycho had installed it long before the Empire took over, when SIs and RIs were commonplace. Before the

Empire, Synthetic Intelligences managed most space stations and even the larger non-military ships—bulk freighters, colony ships, and the like.

When the Empire took over and moved in, they determined that removing the Tycho station RI would be too problematic and not worth the effort. So, it remained in charge of inventory, cargo manifests and shipping routes, and traffic control.

Skip tricked it into a recursion loop that he was certain would keep it occupied and unaware of his and Rudy's presence for a few hours. Better yet, if he was right, the RI wouldn't even know it had been tricked, or that they had spent time sifting through the station computer records.

They really don't treat it well, Ruby observed, running through some comm logs from the command center.

What did you expect? The Empire doesn't like droids or any type of Synthetic Intelligence. The station mind is lucky they didn't delete it, Skip replied. He was looking through cargo manifests to see if the mystery number from Captain Abano's data module matched anything. *I have not found anything. Have you?*

Rudy was silent for a few milliseconds, which, to Skip, felt like he was being ignored by his friend. Finally, Rudy said, *I think I have something.*

CHAPTER 11

"I might explode." Jax patted his stomach. They were walking out of the Wuhan Palace. He was holding a large bag containing their leftovers.

Naomi came up behind him. "That was good. Possibly some of the best I've had." Jax nodded his agreement. She added, "I wonder if they'd be open to a franchise on Kelso?"

Jax nodded absently as he looked at his gPhone screen. "There's a Space Tech here."

"So?" Naomi stepped out of the entry to allow a family of blonde-haired Swedes, judging by their accents, to enter the restaurant.

Jax turned to her. "So. They might have something that will help Baxter. Maybe replacement sub-processors. They deal in old tech as well as new."

Naomi put a hand on his shoulder. "He's nearly thirty years old. They don't make parts."

Jax shrugged her hand off. "I know that. But they might have something compatible." His eyes were pleading.

Naomi inhaled. "We've got time to kill." She smiled. "Lead the way." She fell in behind him as he headed off.

The Space Tech occupied what would have been three storefronts, six levels below Wuhan Palace. Where Spacer Wares, the parent company of Space Tech, sold some of everything, Space Tech sold only electronics. Parts for starships, computers, handheld entertainment devices, gPhones, and tablets of all shapes, sizes, and capabilities? Space Tech sold it. Socks? Head to Spacer Wares.

As the large glass doors slid open, an older woman looked up from her terminal. "Good afternoon, folks. Anything I can help you find?"

Jax consulted his gPhone, then looked up at the woman. "Yeah, we're looking for sub-processor arrays, or something comparable, for a Stellar Dynamics Model Nine combat droid."

The woman's eyes widened. "Well." She rubbed her chin. "That's a pretty old model and," she leaned in, "you know how the Empire is about droids." Jax and Naomi leaned in and nodded to her. She straightened and pointed. "Follow me. No promises, but let's see." She turned and headed off at a surprisingly quick pace for a person her age. The two fell in behind her, hurrying to catch and keep up.

The sales associate looked over her shoulder. "So, you a collector or something?"

Jax had been looking at the shelves as they passed, and turned his attention forward. "What now?"

"Collector? The droid parts. That's a pretty old model of droid. What, thirty or so years? They shut Stellar Dynamics down just after the war. No need for a company that only made droids, after all."

"Oh, collector? Something like that," Jax said. He looked at Naomi and made a face. Probably not a good idea to advertise he had a functional—sort of—combat droid on his ship.

The woman stopped and turned. Before her was shelf after shelf of parts, mostly all covered by a thin layer of dust. "This section," she said, waving to take in the entire aisle, "is the spare parts and trade-ins area. If we have something that will work for your relic, it'll be here." She turned to Jax. "The downside is that it's a bit unregulated. I don't know if there's anything here that will help." She shrugged.

Naomi groaned. Jax nodded. "Thank you." As the woman walked away, he turned to his partner. "Well, you wanted to be part of this."

Her eyes narrowed. "I meant the profit. Not the digging through dusty bins for parts."

"You take the good, you take the bad..." Jax said in a singsong voice. He pointed to a large bin that had processor-looking things in it. "That one is yours."

Jax looked at his hands. A blackish, oily dust covered them. He growled. "Damnit." He slammed a palm on a shelf, causing a small bucket of older model encryption cards to bounce and rattle.

Naomi, sitting cross-legged on the deck, a bin in front of her, looked up at him. Her nose had a black smudge across it. "What?"

"This is getting us know nowhere."

She struck a sympathetic look. "You knew it was a long shot."

He shrugged. "Yeah. I just figured as busy as this station is, the odds might be in our favor."

She extended an arm, waving to take in the bins they had not yet investigated on that aisle alone. "We're not done."

From somewhere closer to the front of the store, the distinct sound of Imperial shock trooper armor rattling against itself echoed. Jax and Naomi both looked in the sound's direction, the latter standing, brushing her palms on her pants, leaving black smudges.

She looked at Jax. "Was that...?"

"Shock trooper armor? Yeah." He crept toward the end of the aisle that was closer to the front of the store. He leaned out and quickly leaned back. "Shit," he hissed. He moved to let Naomi peer past the end of the aisle. She swore as well. What looked like a full squadron of shock troopers was milling around the entrance.

Naomi picked up the bin she had been rummaging through, tossing in two bits of tech that she had set aside as maybe-potentially-working-after-being-modified, and said, "Think they're here for us?" She put the bin back on a shelf.

Jax shrugged. "Hell if I know. It's not illegal to own an old combat droid." He frowned. "I think. Right?" Naomi shrugged. He glared in the general direction of the front of the store. "That old woman sold us out, though, that's for damn sure." He turned and flipped off the general direction of the checkout area. "I hope they send me a survey about my shopping experience."

Before they could leave the aisle, a man in a fastidiously kept Imperial uniform stepped in to block it. He was tall and thin, his jet-black hair slicked back and held in place with enough product to patch a hole in the station's hull. A pencil-thin mustache looked like a child slashed his face with a marker. Jax looked over his shoulder and saw two shock troopers step into place at the opposite end of the aisle. He whispered, "They're here for us." The look Naomi gave him made it clear she already knew that.

"Hello, citizens," the lanky officer said. His voice was at least a few octaves deeper than it looked like it should be capable of going. "I am Lieutenant Ardoin." Jax and Naomi stared at the lieutenant, assuming he had more to say. When the silence became obviously awkward, the lieutenant coughed. "Yes, well. I understand you're looking for parts of an older model combat droid." It wasn't a question.

Jax figured there wasn't any point in lying. "We are." He pointed to a few of the bins. "No luck here. You wouldn't happen to know where we could find parts somewhere else on the station, would you?"

"I...no," the scarecrow-like officer stammered. "I'd like to know more about your unit. I'm something of a collector myself. I might be interested in taking it off your hands."

Naomi looked at the man, then looked over her shoulder. "You brought a lot of muscle to have a friendly chat about collecting old bots."

Ardoin extended his arms in both directions. "Trapping of rank, I'm afraid." He grinned. "Perhaps you'd like to see my collection?"

Naomi arched an eyebrow. "Do we have a choice?"

"Not really, no." Ardoin grinned, his thin little mustache arching. "I so rarely meet other collectors." He turned, inclined his head, and made his way to the front of the store. The two shock troopers at the other end of the aisle started toward Jax and Naomi, ensuring that they would follow the officer.

As they walked past the checkout area, Jax eyed the sales associate and mouthed the words *sell out* at her. She winked.

The walk from the Space Tech store to the rented commercial space of Lieutenant Ardoin was faster than it should have been, thanks to the shock troopers escorting the party. The lanky lieutenant kept a sizable space, likely at a discount or free, in a tower almost exactly opposite the one they parked the *Osprey* in.

"This is far," Jax quipped under his breath. Naomi elbowed him.

The obviously proud lieutenant turned to face his guests, his back to a nondescript hatch. "I'm so excited to be able to share my collection with people who will appreciate it."

Jax put on his fakest smile. "We can't wait."

Naomi said, "We're...he's not exactly a —" Jax elbowed her.

Jax and Naomi's earpieces crackled. Over the shared comm channel, Rudy said. "We think we figured it out." When neither replied, "Hello? This thing on?"

Ardoin turned and pressed his palm to the access panel set next to the hatch. With a happy beep, the panel turned green. Jax looked at Naomi, shrugging minutely. She glanced around to see where their escorts were standing and planted a finger against her ear and the small, hard-to-detect commset tucked into her ear canal. Her fingertip pulsed blue as she accessed the device's firmware.

We're a bit tied up but will get away as soon as we can. Send details to gPhones.

Aboard the *Osprey*, Rudy's head spun. He said out loud, "Glad we hurried."

"Indeed," Skip agreed. He sent all the information that he and Rudy had collected about the mystery number from Abano's data archive to Jax and Naomi's gPhones.

Naomi followed Jax, who followed an excited Lieutenant Ardoin into his sanctuary. The shock troopers did not follow, taking up positions on either side of the hatch as it slid closed.

"Tada," the excited Imperial officer said as row after row of light strips came to life, bathing the large space in harsh white light.

Jax's mouth hung open. The space was almost twice the size of the mechanical bay he owned on Kelso station. Shelves lined all four walls, two or three rows deep, reaching floor to ceiling. In the center of the cavernous room, a fully intact Sparrow class strike fighter sat on its landing gear. The fighter looked like it had just rolled off the assembly line.

Lieutenant Ardoin ushered them further inside his sanctum. He pointed to the right. "Over there is my collection of handheld weapons." He moved his arm. "Droids in common use pre-Empire."

Jax ran a hand through his hair and said, "Uh, yeah. Do you have a combat droid? Do you have the parts I'm looking for?"

Ardoin turned toward the droid section, motioning for Jax and Naomi to follow. They passed a section of shelving that was packed with mannequins in Independent Systems Alliance military uniforms: everything from naval ensign to admiral, marine to explosive ordnance disposal tech and fighter pilot.

Naomi ran a hand along the nearest shelf. "This is quite the collection."

"Thank you," Ardoin said over his shoulder. "It's taken me years to assemble it. Most of my colleagues don't understand, but history just really speaks to me." He turned toward another aisle. "Here we are."

Both sides of the aisle were full of Baxters. "Holy…" Jax trailed off, taking in the sight. There wasn't a single intact droid. Some were missing a limb or were riddled with plasma burn holes. Four were missing all or part of their heads.

Ardoin frowned. "I'm afraid you won't find what you're looking for here. Finding intact or even mostly intact combat droids has been one of my ongoing frustrations. The Indies threw everything they had at us in their last moments." He gestured to the ravaged metal bodies on both sides of the aisle.

While Jax and Ardoin talked, Naomi moved to another section of the aisle, this one full of smaller droids. She spotted three that were identical to Rudy. She saw a blue and white model that looked a generation or two newer than Rudy, probably one of the last models created. It had a silver dome for a head and no apparent arms. All the nav droids appeared to be in good to excellent condition.

"Perhaps I could purchase the unit you have?" Ardoin asked while Jax was examining one of the more intact combat units—intact except for the multiple fist-sized holes in the torso, some going all the way through.

Jax turned. "What? Oh, no, sorry. My…unit isn't for sale."

Naomi turned back to the two men as the scarecrow-limbed Imperial officer tugged at his sleeves. He said, "Come now. Everything is for sale for the right price." His grin turned decidedly less friendly. He added, "I can be quite persuasive."

Naomi eyed the pair, then said, "You know, I'd love to see

that Sparrow. It's intact?" She batted her eyelashes in what she hoped was a seductive manner.

Her request had the desired effect of breaking the silent stalemate that was developing between Jax and the lieutenant.

Ardoin turned, clearing his throat. "Oh, yes. One of my most prized possessions." He ushered them out of the aisle toward the center of the space and the starfighter parked there.

CHAPTER 12

The Sparrow class strike fighter was, at the time, the pinnacle of modern combat engineering, marrying a Rudimentary Intelligence to the pilot's control harness. The combination made the nimble craft incredibly dangerous. The Unity Militia came to hate the craft.

While Lieutenant Ardoin circled the antique starfighter, explaining every piece of equipment, Naomi was scanning the room as best she could, looking for anything to use as a distraction so she and Jax could make their exit and get on with salvaging the Nemesis Fleet and being rich. In her head, she'd already spent a sizeable chunk of the expected salvage money they'd get from the fleet of old warships. She unconsciously rubbed her palms together as she looked around. Finally, when the two men moved to the other side of the craft, she ducked back down an aisle, out of sight.

"It took me three months, and in the end, a squad of shock troopers paying a visit, to secure the port engine," Ardoin said, resting a hand on the engine's thrust novel. "She was mostly intact when I got her, sans the port engine and the flight computer. I decided to skip the computer. No need for an annoying droid intelligence I'd only be shutting down anyway."

Even without the RI, the fighter could be lethal. The Sparrow class strike fighter was the workhorse of the Independent Systems Alliance fleet. Able to launch from a ship or planetary base and deliver blistering missile attacks, the nimble single occupant craft often made the difference between a win or a loss in the early days of the war.

Jax was nodding along, watching the annoying Imperial show off his toy. It had become clear that the man, while sometimes paying for his treasures, often resorted to bullying and using the full force of his position on Tycho to take what he wanted from people.

As Jax and Ardoin came back around the nose of the craft, Naomi appeared back from where she had ducked out of sight. "You have quite the treasure trove, Lieutenant," she purred. Jax looked at her appraisingly.

"Thank you, dear." The man nodded before turning once more to Jax. "Now, about your combat droid..."

Before Jax could reply, a cacophony rose from several aisles away. Frantic beeps and whistles were followed by a choir of voices shouting expletives in numerous languages.

Ardoin spun. "What in the blazes..." A yellow nav droid, similar in design to Rudy, shot into the open area where the star fighter was parked, crashing into the side of the vehicle. It was beeping and screeching frantically, its thin metal arms cartwheeling as it ricocheted off the fighter.

A second later, two more droids appeared, one swearing up a storm in Egyptian, while the other unit used German and English interchangeably. Both raced toward the trio of humans, then spun off down separate aisles.

Ardoin spun around. "This is—what is—Guards!" he finally shouted. He turned to address Jax when the blue and white droid that Naomi had seen earlier barreled into him. It got around on two legs that ended in wheels, with a third that deployed from its cylindrical body. It was beeping and whistling in a way that made it clear to all around that it was not saying nice things. It knocked Ardoin over before vanishing down another aisle.

The hatch opened, followed by the augmented shouts of shock troopers.

Ardoin turned and bolted toward the hatch. "Don't let them out!" he shouted, arms flailing. One of the droids made for the hatch. It exploded when several high energy rounds struck it. "Don't destroy them!" the lieutenant shrieked.

Jax and Naomi fell in behind him, the former looking at his partner, eyebrow raised. The Japanese woman smiled but said nothing. When they caught up to Ardoin, the man was shouting orders.

"We'll just see ourselves out," Naomi said. The Imperial man barely registered her comment as he waved a dismissive hand. A purple nav droid on which someone had painted a smiley face raced past, beeping and shouting obscenities in Spanish.

The hatch ground closed behind them as Jax tapped his earpiece. "Rudy? Skip? We're clear."

"About time," the *Osprey*'s SI replied. "What were you doing?"

"Not important," Jax answered.

Rudy cut in. "Head to the main spaceport commons. Central hub, Deck 19."

"Copy that," Naomi said. She looked up and down the corridor to get her bearings, then pointed. "This way."

Jax nodded and fell in next to her. They did not want to attract attention, so they kept their pace to a fast walk.

While the lift they found whisked them toward the nearest

spoke and back to the hub, Jax asked, "What was all that back there?"

Naomi grinned. "His combat droids were a mess. But all those nav droids, they were just powered down. He had restraining bolts on them all, but," she held up both hands, her fingers pulsing with blue light, "they weren't much of a match for me. The droids were irate once I explained the situation."

Jax laughed. "Damn." Naomi nodded. "I feel bad—he's going to recapture those poor bots and lock 'em up again," Jax added.

Naomi's face turned serious. "He will, but I embedded some routines that would at least allow the droids to communicate with each other even after the restraining bolts are reattached."

Jax laughed again, this time planting his hands on his knees. "Okay, that's clever." He said between deep breaths.

Naomi didn't look over but asked, "Why didn't you just tell him you're not a collector?"

Jax turned, a sly grin creasing his face. "None of his business."

Naomi sighed but said nothing in reply.

The lift doors slid open.

"Where to?"

"The rental lockers," Skip answered.

"Locker 8675309," Rudy added.

As Tycho station grew, facilities moved from place to place, keeping up with renovations. While station operations had moved to the command towers at the top of the hub, public-facing facilities mostly remained where they had been installed. Deck 19 was one such section: lodging, rentable by the hour; restrooms, complete with showers, free for anyone to use; more quick eats stalls than could be easily counted. And in the center of the deck, a sea of rentable lockers, from units small enough to hold only a gPhone to units that Jax was pretty sure he could squeeze into. They filled concentric, circular rows covering the entire center of the deck. There were hundreds of them. A tween deck mezzanine had hundreds more.

They only needed to find one.

"I feel like an idiot. Are these in some order I don't understand?" Jax groused. He was scanning up and down the columns of lockers with his finger.

From the other side of the aisle, Naomi said, "Just look at the top row. It should be in the top row."

Jax blushed. "Oh. How do you know that?" He adjusted his approach.

They got to the end of the aisle and Jax slowed down just enough so that Naomi would lead the way to the next row. She looked over her shoulder and smirked as he followed.

Halfway down the next aisle, Jax shouted, "Hey, I got it!" He looked around, hunching over a bit. He waved Naomi over. The locker was one of the smaller ones, barely big enough for a tablet.

Jax stepped aside as Naomi put her hand on the locking mechanism. These lockers were holdovers from the days when smugglers, and worse, would leave dead drops for associates. When the Empire took over the station, and the more illicit trades moved on, there was no reason to remove the vast sea of lockers. Spacers still used the inexpensive storage as a way to keep a few pairs of clean clothes in different stations without the burden of renting a living space.

A moment later, the locking mechanism beeped, and the small door swung open. Jax leaned in to get a look and was shoved back by Naomi. She reached in and removed a folded piece of paper. She held the paper out to Jax, who took it. "I swear to God, I hate scavenger hunts," Naomi ground out.

Jax shrugged. "At least it's not another encrypted data module." She looked at him flatly. He looked past her. "There's some seating over there by the boba joint."

By the time Naomi sat down, Jax was drumming his fingers on the tabletop. He had the folded paper in the middle of the table. He glared as she sat. "What?" she demanded. "I wanted a drink." She sat the milky white and brown drink down on the table, tapioca balls swishing gently at the bottom. Two hot dogs joined the drink. "And I was hungry." She slid one of the hot dogs over to Jax.

"Whatever," Jax said, grabbing one of the hot dogs. He unfolded the paper, once, then again, until the full sheet lay between them. It was standard printer paper, not that such things existed much anymore.

"Where did he get printer paper?" Jax wondered aloud.

Whomever Abano had hired for this part of his little breadcrumb project had gone old school. The paper held a single set of coordinates, written by someone with terrible penmanship. "Someone needs to work on his or her handwriting," Jax said. He studied the coordinates, then looked at Naomi. "Anything?" She sipped her drink, tapioca balls racing up the clear the straw. "No. But then, I'm not a nav droid. Send a pic to the boys." She sat the drink down and grabbed her hotdog, taking a bite, mustard dribbling onto the table.

Jax looked at the yellow glob and frowned. She was right. That would have made more sense. He snapped a pic with his gPhone, sending it to Rudy and Skip. He then crumpled the paper into a ball. While he waited for Skip and Rudy, he finished his hotdog.

"They're coordinates," Skip said over the encrypted channel they all shared.

Naomi raised her eyebrows, noisily slurping tiny tapioca balls up her straw.

"Yeah. We know that. Where?" Jax demanded. He reached for Naomi's drink, snapping his fingers. She made a face and finished the drink off.

"Oh," Skip said. "I suppose you did."

Rudy jumped in. "Deep space. Sector 12 by 42 by 17."

"Anything there?" Naomi asked.

"Beats me," the ship's navigator replied. "Nothing in the star charts. It is a bit above the galactic plane, so, again...beats me," he repeated.

Skip chipped in, "The last entry in the Wikigalaxia navigation database is almost forty years old."

Naomi looked at Jax, then the piece of archaic paper. "Curiouser and curiouser."

Jax stood and tossed the crumpled-up piece of paper into a nearby matter recycling receptacle. He nodded to Naomi. "Let's go." They walked toward the nearest lift.

"Oh, wait. Jax!" Naomi said as they passed in front of a boutique offering women's fashions.

"Really?" Jax looked at her, then at the boutique. There were a few folks inside, looking around.

Naomi didn't answer. She walked in, heading straight for the summer dresses.

Jax made an exaggerated sigh and followed her. Walking in, he spotted a pair of women looking at swimwear. He changed course, heading toward them. "I like the blue one," he offered.

Naomi looked up from the dress she was holding to watch him. She huffed and went back to browsing.

The two women looked up. The blonde said, "Uh, thanks. We didn't ask." They turned and moved to another rack.

Naomi walked behind him and whispered, "Burn." She had two sun dresses under her arm.

Before Jax could reply, Skip said, "Captain, your friend is trying to find me."

Jax moved to the back corner of the store, near the fitting rooms. He put a finger to his ear. "What? What do you mean?"

"I've been monitoring the station's network and found a search query running against the station's security system. It was looking for your face. Yours and Naomi's."

Jax looked around the store. The two women from the swimwear section were making their way to the fitting rooms, just a few feet from where Jax had posted up. One mumbled, "Creep," as they walked by.

Jax blushed and moved to the other side of the small shop. He and Naomi were the only other customers. A bored-looking teenage boy was behind the counter playing a game on his gPhone. "Have they back tracked to the docking area yet?"

"Not that I can tell."

"Can you scrub the data? Or spoof it?" He snapped his fingers to get Naomi's attention. When she looked up, he pointed to his ear.

Naomi nodded and tapped her ear, joining the conversation. "What's up?"

Jax let Skip fill Naomi in, then said, "We gotta get off station."

"I told ya you shoulda just said you weren't a collector. That beanpole idiot thinks Skip is full of treasure."

"Treasure?" Skip asked.

"Long story," Jax said. He added, "See if you can wipe Naomi and me leaving the ship and going through customs. That should create enough of a gap that he won't easily find you."

"I'll see what I can do," the *Osprey*'s SI replied.

"Play that back," Lieutenant Ardoin said, pointing at the screen. He was leaning over a junior officer in the secondary command center, watching a security recording from Deck 19, just outside the boba shop near the lockers. On the screen was the pair he had intended to take a combat droid from.

After he and his squad recaptured the errant navigation droids, he ordered his people in the secondary command center to trace his mysterious guests through the station. He had assumed they'd make for their ship, allowing him to order them detained. His plan had been to fabricate some contraband, have their ship impounded, and take whatever he wanted off it. Instead, they had gone to the lockers.

Ardoin was certain the combat droid and who knew what other pre-Imperial trinkets would be aboard the younger man's ship. He did not know either of their names but felt certain they were fellow collectors.

"Zoom in," he ordered. The image enlarged, then focused on Naomi's face. Ardoin looked at the young woman. "On. The. Paper."

The young woman's cheeks burned. "Sorry, sir." The image shifted to the paper between the two people at the table. On it, clear as day, was a set of scribbled stellar coordinates.

"Send a screen grab of this to my tablet." Ardoin stood and made for the exit. "Then delete the footage."

The young officer looked up. "Sir, shouldn't we alert the station commander?"

Ardoin looked over his shoulder. "Rest assured, Ensign. Security services will brief the commander on this. You do your job, I'll do mine."

The younger woman pursed her lips, running a hand over her dark hair, pulled into a regulation bun. "Of course, sir. Sorry, sir."

Ardoin smiled and continued toward the hatch that led to

the security office. He stopped. "Remember to erase the footage, Ensign."

"Yes, sir," the young officer called. She turned back to her console and keyed in the command to erase the footage of Jax and Naomi finding the coordinates to the next leg of their journey, and the first leg of Lieutenant Ardoin's.

In his office, Lieutenant Ardoin pulled his tablet out of the desk drawer. Waking it, he saw the ensign had sent the image as ordered. A quick scan through the security feeds confirmed she had indeed deleted the original recording. He dropped into his seat and accessed the station communication network. Then, he accessed his private directory and a contact entry that he kept encrypted within his encrypted directory.

The Empire allowed the Tycho station RI to continue existing, managing traffic and station systems, but all around it, they had erected the standard Imperial computer operating systems. Any Imperial officer anywhere knew how to operate the system. Ardoin tapped an icon, placing the call. Officers like Ardoin knew how to back door calls so that the communication system did not log them.

After a minute of waiting, he was about to abort the call when the screen switched from the black screen to a groggy man with a missing eye. "What?"

"Get your people together. I have a job for you."

The other man rubbed his stubble-covered jaw. "What kind

of job? We're still stripping that colony transport you pointed us to."

"One that's worth your time. It'll make the payoff from that old colony hauler look like spare change. Come to Tycho. I'm going with you on this one."

The one-eyed man growled. He reached off screen and placed an eye patch over the empty socket. "This better be worth it."

Ardoin grinned. "I think it will be." He closed the connection and said to himself, "If he has a functional combat droid, he must have much more, either on his ship, or wherever he's going." The Imperial amateur treasure hunter was already thinking of the expansion to his collection chamber. He could part with a few pieces to fund it. A few more to cover some of his expenses and keep his superiors from asking questions. He'd need to force the tenants out of the units below his, but that was fine.

Lieutenant Ardoin tapped a different icon on his tablet. "Sergeant Baynes. I have an assignment for your squad. Off the books."

Ardoin had spent years finding officers and grunts that were open to his side projects. Baynes had signed on shortly after her transfer to Tycho. According to her record, it was a last chance posting after punching her previous commander in the face. Ardoin had transferred her to his security division after making sure she'd be open to side projects.

Jax looked out the front windows of the boutique and spotted a group of shock troopers. One had sergeant stripes on the shoulder pauldron. The group was coming from the direction of the tables Jax and Naomi had recently vacated.

"Shit," he hissed.

Naomi turned, and when she saw the troopers, she crouched behind the rack of clothes she was next to. She looked at Jax, placing the sun dresses she was going to try on, on the rack next to her. "We gotta get back to the ship."

Jax raised an eyebrow. "Ya think?" He watched the shock troopers walk into a stall. "Let's go." He headed for the exit, Naomi on his heels.

They crept out of the boutique in the opposite direction the team of shock troopers had come from.

Jax tapped his ear. "Skip, one more job. This one is a bit pressing."

"Because keeping your weird Imperial friend from finding me isn't pressing?"

Jax groaned. "Okay, something equally pressing. We've got shock troopers, probably looking for us. Guessing they're in the security feeds. Can you get in and scrub us?"

There was a pause, then Skip asked, "Like in real time?"

"I guess. Yeah?"

Skip made a sigh-like sound. The comm channel beeped.

Jax looked over his shoulder. "We might need your..." He wiggled his fingers at her.

Naomi made a face. "That means we need to get to a station systems terminal." She looked around. "I doubt there are any on the purely public levels."

Jax nodded his agreement. "The level below this one. It's mostly mechanical. No public space." He pointed to a door along the bulkhead a hundred or so meters away. It had the universal illustration of a staircase on it. "That hatch."

A trio of spacers was walking the direction Jax and Naomi needed. They fell in with them, laughing at the joke one of the dark-skinned group had just made. A woman with her hair done in intricately patterned cornrows looked at the new arrivals. "Who you?"

Jax looked at her. "Just a pair of spacers using you all for cover."

The woman looked where Jax's gaze had settled and saw the quartet of shock troopers moving to a new commercial shop, a women's clothing boutique. She looked at Jax, grinning. One of her front teeth was gold. "Aye." She winked, draping an arm around Jax. She said something in Arabic, eliciting laughter from her comrades.

Reaching the hatch, Jax nodded to the New Egyptian spacers and pressed the release to open the hatch. Naomi followed him through the hatch.

CHAPTER 13

The stairwell was empty. The deck below the shopping area and public lockers was exactly as Jax said. Enormous pieces of equipment hummed, rumbled, chugged, and whined as they provided protein, water, power, and other necessities to the above shops and food stalls.

Naomi's gaze cast about the area. "Okay. Any ideas where a terminal would be?"

"There's gotta be a break room or something," Jax answered. He set off toward the middle of the space. "There's always a storage or break room on these levels. Even if it wasn't part of the original plans. Station workers are great at improvising." He looked around. "There's a break room."

They walked for a while until Jax said, "There." He pointed to a structure made of pre-fabricated pieces of internal hull plating. Each piece looked to have been attached to the next with spray epoxy. Fasteners held the makeshift walls to the various pipes and conduits in the ceiling.

"That looks... ramshackle," Naomi said dubiously as they approached.

"Like I said. Station workers are masters of improvising. If this wasn't here, they'd have to go back to central operations for their breaks and lunch, wasting a ton of time—time that comes out of their breaks."

He grinned. "This way, they bring their meal, store it here during the shift, and take their break in situ." He shrugged. "People like these raised me after my folks died."

He pushed open the door and said, "Well, shit."

Naomi looked over his shoulder to make eye contact with a heavyset Asian woman, her gray hair pulled into a tight bun, held in place with twin pieces of metal that might have been pieces of a cooling unit.

"Who the hell are you two?" the woman demanded. "I thought you were going to stand out there yacking like idiots all afternoon." She snapped her fingers. Two goons that Jax hadn't noticed stepped in from either side of the door and put a hand on his and Naomi's shoulders.

"Oh. Uh…You're not station workers," Jax stammered.

"Mōshiwakearimasen," Naomi said. She shrugged the hand on her shoulder off and bowed.

The woman squinted at Naomi. She stood and walked around her desk to stand face to face with Naomi. At least as close to face to face as possible. The portly older woman was a full head shorter than Naomi. "Where do you come from?"

"Kel—" Jax started to answer but fell silent at the side-eyed glance shot his way by Naomi.

"Shinchaku Hokkaido," Naomi answered. She added, "My grandparents emigrated."

The other woman nodded slowly. She made a minute gesture, and the two men released her and Jax and returned to their positions flanking the door. "Something tells me you didn't come to this level looking for us." She looked at Jax, eyebrow arched.

He stared at her until he was sure she meant for him to speak. "Oh. No, we didn't. I figured there would be a terminal down here. I knew that station workers would have built a break room somewhere on this deck. I figured there were good odds they'd have put a terminal in so they could listen to the station feed."

"What you want a terminal for?" The old woman leaned toward Jax.

Jax glanced at Naomi and chewed his lip for a moment. "We're trying to avoid station security. This lanky lieutenant with a fetish for pre-Empire crap—"

"Ardoin," the woman interrupted.

Jax pointed at her. "That's the one. He thinks our ship is full of pre-Empire memorabilia or something. Decided I'm a collector like him. A rival, I guess."

"Is it? Your ship, full of trinkets?" She moved to sit back down behind her desk. The chair's hydraulics whined under her weight as she settled in.

"No. I have a friend, a combat droid. He's—"

"Your friend is a combat mech?" the woman, whom Jax was fairly certain was some type of crime boss, interrupted again. She leaned forward, her hands folded in front of her on the desk.

Jax sighed. "Yeah. He's damaged. We thought there might be parts here, given Tycho's history and size."

"Not a terrible assumption. You're the ones beanpole hassled at Space Tech?" Both of her maybe-prisoners nodded. "He's got about a third of the shock trooper garrison in his pocket. The station commander doesn't know, as far I can tell. She's pretty clueless."

She pinned Jax with a stare. "And the terminal?"

"Uh." Jax cleared his throat. "She's really good with computers. We thought we could insert a virus that kept the security system from seeing us while we made our way back to our ship."

"And then walk to your ship and depart," the mobster woman said, completing the thought. Jax nodded. "Maybe I can help. For a price."

While Tycho station's RI handled most of the shipping and traffic logistics, running the massive station still required an op center that took up most of the command tower. The levels below the multi-tiered, bowl-shaped space were administrative offices for lower-level functionaries. They reserved the levels above the ops center for senior officers and visiting superiors.

The ops center was ringed by floor-to-ceiling transparent hull panels, affording staffers a view of the station and surrounding space in all directions.

"Commander Argent, ma'am," Lieutenant Ardoin said, stepping up the raised command platform at the bottom of the wide circular command center. "You sent for me?" Around them on successive levels, officers went about their business managing the vast station. From the platform, the commander had a view of nearly every monitor in the space.

The commanding officer of Tycho station was a stately woman in her mid-fifties. Her age would be impossible to tell from looking at her, though. She kept herself in tip-top shape and made sure her skin, thanks to countless experimental regimens, was clear and smooth.

She had been commander of Tycho station for nearly the entirety of its time under Imperial rule. Ardoin found her breathtakingly gorgeous and, to his liking, oblivious to his side interests. Calling her head of security to the ops center was unusual.

Commander Argent turned. "Lieutenant Ardoin, thank you. The RI flagged some unusual queries coming from the secondary command post. Normally I'd ignore it, but the watch stander," she gestured to a terminal next to where they were standing and the young officer occupying the seat in front of it, "felt it warranted attention."

Ardoin cursed the ensign for not passing his requested queries through an anonymizing filter. He'd deal with her later. Leaning over to examine the screen, he looked up at his commanding officer, smiling. "Ah, yes. A station resident came to me yesterday. An unscrupulous spacer robbed her of her life savings by pretending to be a wealthy investor looking for clients." He shrugged. "Hard to believe anyone falls for Ponzi schemes anymore, but here we are."

The older woman nodded along. "I see. Terrible. And...?"

Ardoin nodded. "And, I offered to use my authority to attempt to track him through the security cameras back to his ship so that we could lock it down before he could escape with her money."

The commander smiled. "I see. Very well, continue. You're a good man, Ardoin. A credit to the Empire."

Ardoin bowed his head. "Thank you, Commander." He turned on his heel and strode toward the bank of lifts.

⌒

"What kind of help?" Naomi asked.

"What kind of price?" Jax added.

The other woman smiled. "The kind you need and a fair price." She shrugged. "Mostly fair." Holding both hands out in front of her, palms up, she added, "I could, of course, place a call to station security. Or maybe directly to the annoying lieutenant?"

Jax held up a hand. "Okay, okay, don't get testy. We're docked in Tower 8."

The woman motioned one of her men over. After whispering in his ear for a bit, the man left. She turned to Jax and Naomi. "I can get you there, off the grid. You won't show up on a single camera."

Jax nodded. "Price?"

The woman grinned. "I know you. Did you know that? That you're famous in certain circles?"

Jax and Naomi looked at each other. The former shrugged. "Uh...no."

"Jackson Caruso and his business partner, Naomi Himura. You may not have gotten the credit, but in the circles I run in, it's well known that you two are responsible for the nearly complete destruction of Crimson Orchid along with several other syndicates and cartels." She tilted her head, eyeing Jax. "I thought your hair would be longer. Like Norse god."

Jax frowned. "Uh...okay." He unconsciously ran a hand through his hair. "That's an incredibly detailed misconception."

The mobster woman waved a hand, dismissing the topic. "My organization has had rather good fortunes since that whole thing on Columbiana."

Jax shrugged. "So, this on the house? Show of appreciation?"

The woman tittered, putting a thick-fingered hand to her mouth. "Oh, no, dear boy. I'm appreciative, not stupid. The price is a favor. To be called in later."

"Oh man. I hate those," Jax groaned.

Naomi nudged him, then turned to their potential savior. "Deal."

The door opened again, and a wiry, dark-skinned boy entered. The woman said, "Follow Stanley."

Jax looked at the boy. "Stanley?"

The boy nodded. "Hi. Dick."

Naomi did her best to stifle the chuckle.

Jax scowled, tipped his head, then looked at the older woman. "I didn't catch your name. I should probably know whom I owe a favor to."

The woman smiled and motioned for Stanley to take them out of her office.

Stanley led them through a maze of equipment, away from the mysterious gangster woman's office.

"So, Stanley," Naomi said. "What's your boss's name? We didn't catch it."

The younger man reached what looked like a dead end between two massive protein sequencers. He pressed a section of hull plating that looked like the rest. A panel slid aside. He turned. "She doesn't tell strangers her name." He looked Naomi, then Jax, up and down. "You two definitely count as strange." He crawled into the dark opening.

Jax and Naomi were staring at the hole when the young man's head emerged. "Coming?" They crawled in, one after the other.

"You know where you're going?" Jax asked the boy.

Stanley ran a hand over his close-cropped curls of blue hair. "Docking Tower 8, right?"

"Yeah," Jax said.

While Jax and Naomi followed their young guide—climbing ladders, straddling pipes, wading through murky water, and more—Jax tapped his earpiece. "Rudy, Skip. Sitrep?"

Skip answered, "I could scrub only some of the security footage before someone noticed I was in the system. We had to release the station's RI and pull back."

Naomi cut in. "Will Ardoin be able to find you?"

"I don't think so. I am certain I scrubbed your disembarkation. He'll probably be able to narrow down what docking tower we're in, though."

"That's good, -ish. We're..." Jax paused and looked at Stanley. "How long?"

The blue-haired teen turned. "About an hour."

"An hour?" Naomi whined.

Jax turned his attention back to Skip. "We're an hour out."

"No rush," Rudy quipped.

Jax scowled and closed the connection. He tapped Stanley. "So, what's your story?"

"Short, if I tell you anything," the young man replied, the whites of his brown eyes bright. He pointed to the right. A meter-diameter duct ran off into the distance. He put his hand on an access panel. "This runs along the top of the spoke. It's the secondary heat transfer duct. It's gonna be uncomfortable."

Jax made a face. "I'm pretty sure we waded through shit back there. I think we can take muggy."

The other man shrugged and slid open an access panel. A burst of steam erupted from the opening. "Last one through, close that up." He didn't wait for an answer, kneeling down and crawling into the duct.

Naomi and Jax crawled in after their guide, the latter taking up the rear. He looked around the space, then slid the panel closed. The heat transfer duct was indeed muggy. Sweat began pouring out of them.

"Nothing yet, sir," Sergeant Baynes said. She and her squad had checked every commercial stall on Deck 19. The woman that ran one of the clothing boutiques had seen the two targets earlier but couldn't say which direction they had gone when they left.

From his office, Lieutenant Ardoin said, "Interesting. They're certainly clever." He was scrolling through security feeds of the commercial space. "Wait. There."

"Sir?"

Ardoin zoomed in. On the terminal screen, Jax and Naomi were opening a service door.

"Sergeant, they went through Service Hatch B-15."

"Copy that, sir. Up or down?" In a second window, Ardoin watched Baynes and her team march for the service hatch.

The lanky lieutenant tapped his chin. "You'll have to split up. The sensors in the stairwell are out." He made a note on his gPhone to put in the service requisition to get that addressed. Someone had to have disabled those sensors on purpose so that they could move freely around the hub. He wanted to know who.

"Copy that, sir." On the screen, the shock troopers entered the stairwell.

CHAPTER 14

Despite their best efforts, neither Jax nor Naomi had even the slightest success at getting any more details from their teenage guide. No matter what they said or asked, he evaded or simply ignored them. They crept, climbed, crawled, shimmied, and even at one point, swam their way to Docking Tower 8.

Stanley stopped at a metal grate. He looked over his shoulder. "This will get you where you're going. The space dock facility is a mostly closed system. It'd take a while to get through it all. Easier if you walk above ground from here."

Naomi crawled to look past the young man. "That looks like the customs reception area."

"Clearly, you're the brains of the operation." The boy smirked, then flinched when Naomi gave him a look. "It is. You'll have to go through like normal." He raised an eyebrow. "Can you?"

Jax shrugged. "I don't know." He tapped his ear. "Skip. Can you get back into the station's computer, just enough to make sure we pass through customs?"

"One second," the *Osprey*'s SI replied.

Stanley peered at Jax. "You have more people?"

Naomi answered, "Something like that."

In Jax's ear, Skip said, "Okay, you should be clear for at least five minutes."

Jax hissed, "That's not much time." He nodded to Naomi and Stanley, and the former pushed the grate open. "We've got five minutes." He turned to the pale young man. "Thanks. Tell your boss she knows where to find me."

The boy nodded and shimmied around his two charges to vanish back down the way they had come.

Naomi eased out of the crawlspace and looked around. No one was around. "Clear." Jax followed, closing the grate behind him.

Ahead of them, the customs checkpoint was moderately busy. Jax checked his gPhone. It was nearing midnight station time.

They got in line behind a group of taller-than-normal spacers, all with pale blonde hair in bowl cuts. The leader of the group was talking to the customs officer.

Naomi looked at Jax and mouthed the words, *the Dutch*. He rolled his eyes and nodded. He whispered, "Skip, we're almost there. Anything hinky?"

"Negative, Captain. Don't forget to disconnect the data trunk tap."

Jax looked at Naomi and made a face. "Damn, I totally forgot about that." He pointed to the group of Dutch spacers in front of them.

"Me, too," Naomi admitted.

Ahead of them, the Dutch spacers were moving through the checkpoint, having been cleared by the bored-looking customs officer. Jax stepped up to the counter, his current ident pulled up on his gPhone. "Hi," he said to the agent.

The officer looked at the phone screen, then up at Jax. He waved Naomi over and took her gPhone, looking at the screen.

He looked at the screens, then the grime-covered couple before him. He sniffed and wrinkled his nose.

Jax watched the Dutch crew as they sauntered across the deck toward their freighter, laughing and joking with each other.

The customs officer slid both devices back to their owners, his free hand waving the air in front of him. "Here you go. Safe travels."

Jax made a tight-lipped smile. "Thanks." He and Naomi departed the checkpoint.

Naomi broke into her best fast-but-not-obvious walk toward the dock worker locker room she and Jax had visited when they arrived. She tapped her ear and said, "Keep the Dutch busy."

Jax watched her go, then looked at the Dutch, almost to their ship. "What? How?" He sighed when she waved her hand absently. He increased his speed. "Hey, guys!" He waved.

One of the blonde-haired spacers turned. "Ja? Kunnen we je helpen?"

Jax came to a stop. "Ohhhh. Uh..." He spied Naomi reach the dock worker locker room. "I, uh..." He looked around.

"Wat is er mis met deze idioot?" the guy who might have been the captain said, looking around at his people. A few of his crew chuckled. The man who was closest to Jax looked at his captain and shrugged.

"I wanted to ask you all..." He rubbed his palms on his pants. "Have you found Jesus Christ?"

"What?" The captain came forward. "What are you on about?" He looked at his colleagues, all of whom shrugged and shook their heads.

"Uh, yeah. Jesus. Important to, you know, have him in your life. In your corner and stuff."

Naomi emerged from the locker room dressed once again

like a dock worker. She jogged over to the Dutch-flagged freighter.

"What are you? A Mormon?" The captain looked around. "How did you get in here? It is crew only past customs."

Back in a borrowed dock worker vest and matching multi-pocketed pants, Naomi crouched down and crawled under the heavy freighter. She watched Jax talk to the freighter crew and shook her head.

She levered open the deck plate and reached down. A tug on the wire tap did nothing. "Hey, Skip. How do I disconnect this thing?" She pulled on the thick cable again. Nothing.

"Stop tugging on it," Skip said.

Naomi looked around. "How do you—? Never mind." She glanced over toward Jax, who was making hand gestures and shrugging. The Dutch looked like they were losing patience with him.

The *Osprey*'s SI said, "Twist the washer near the cable counter clockwise until you hear a click. Then, pull the cable loose. The tap will stay behind. By the time anyone notices it, we'll be long gone."

Naomi followed the instructions and was rewarded with a soft click. She gave the thick cable a tug, and it popped free of the tap. She closed the access panel all the way and said, "Done. Heading in."

"You look like you slept in garbage," the Dutch freighter captain said. "Leave us alone. Take your religion with you." He turned and gestured to his crew.

Jax could feel the sweat beading on his forehead. "Space is dangerous!" He waved his arms. The crew turned back to look at him, this time with a mix of irritation and pity on all of their faces. He went on, "Every time we go into space, let alone a wormhole, you just never know, right? Why not have Jesus on your side? Or God? I think it's God you want on your side." He tapped his chin. "They're one and the same, yeah?"

The nearest Dutch crewer threw her hands in the air. "He must be drunk."

"Or stoned," one of her colleagues said.

Jax glanced past them to their ship and saw Naomi creeping away. The thick data cable was snaking its way back up into the *Osprey*. He turned to the Dutch spacers and shouted at the top of his lungs. "Jesus saves! God is my co-pilot!" He turned on his heel and stomped back toward the customs checkpoint as slowly as he could. Every eye in the docking area was on him.

The freighter crew exchanged looks, then turned and continued on to their ship. The last of the data cable slithered up the *Osprey*'s boarding ramp. Jax heard the crew laughing at him as they walked up the ramp to their ship. Once they were aboard, he turned and ran toward the *Osprey*.

Naomi was in the cargo hold, still dressed like a dockworker. She turned to Jax as he came up the stairs. "We gotta work on your improv skills." She made a face. "Jesus…? Your co-pilot?"

Jax shrugged and went up the stairs to the common deck.

While Jax and Naomi busied themselves with prepping the *Osprey* for launch, Rudy sent a message to Skip and Baxter.

I have an idea. I know the fabricator can't create the sub-processor stacks you need, but while we were connected to the station, I did a little digging.

Baxter, still in his power cradle in engineering, unable to leave it, sent, *Okay, and?*

Rudy sent a rude emoji then. *That lieutenant that Jax and Naomi met. The collector. His private archive had all kinds of blueprints and design ideas. It took me a bit to find it—he's good at hiding his activities from his superiors. Anyway, he spent a fair amount of time working on designs to keep his collection going as they got older and parts became scarce.* When Baxter sent an angry faced emoji, Rudy continued, *He was working on a design to repair his combat droids. All of them were far too damaged to be of use to you, but one of his ideas was an auxiliary control unit.*

Skip interrupted, *Why are you taking so long to get to the point?*

Rudy sent a flurry of rude emojis. *We can build one with the raw materials we have on hand. It won't be a permanent solution, but it should allow you to move around again, if we add straps to it, make it a backpack.*

Baxter sent, *Why didn't you just say that at the beginning?*

Rudy signed off and set about plotting a course for their latest destination.

On the bridge, Jax looked over his shoulder. "All set?" Naomi, at her station, nodded. He tapped a control. "Tycho station space control, this is the *Parakeet*, requesting departure clearance." Outside the clear viewport, he saw the lumbering bulk of the Dutch freighter glide through the static atmosphere barrier.

"Copy that, *Parakeet*," the space control operator answered. A display to Jax's left lit up with a flight path and clearance code. "*Parakeet*, you're clear to depart. Please don't stray from the path."

As the *Osprey* rose, Jax caught sight of the squad of shock troopers that he and Naomi had seen earlier, pushing their way through the customs screening area into the docking bay proper.

"Time to go," he said, pushing the throttle control forward. The *Osprey* darted through the static atmosphere barrier.

Naomi was feeding the thick data cable into the industrial fabricator's matter recycler when she looked over at Baxter. "You online, big guy?"

The matte black droid remained motionless, but his red optical sensor came alive. "I am."

Naomi smiled. "Good. Rudy told me about his idea for the auxiliary processing unit."

"Did it take him two hours to get to the point?" the tall droid deadpanned.

Naomi fed more of the heavy cable into the hopper. The machinery inside was systematically breaking it down into component elements, sorting and storing it all for future use by the fabricator. She smiled. "He did take a while to get there, yeah." She looked over her shoulder. "Sounds like a workable plan, though, right?"

Baxter inclined his head. "Considering the alternatives, yes."

"You don't sound enthusiastic."

The droid made a noise like he was exhaling. "I came to terms with my functions ceasing." He shrugged.

Naomi fed the last of the cable into the hopper. "Well, once we're underway, Rudy can get started on it." She turned and left the engineering space.

On the bridge, Jax was sitting in his command chair watching the distance from Tycho grow on one of the displays, while watching nearby traffic through the wraparound transparent viewport.

Naomi came up the staircase just as the *Osprey* slid past a bulk freighter that had to be at least three kilometers long. She watched the massive ship pass, her hand on Rudy's flat, rust-colored head. "So."

Jax looked over his shoulder. "So." He broke into a grin. "Now we get rich."

Tycho station kept strict rules regarding how close to the station and traffic lanes a ship could open a wormhole. The gravitational shear caused by an opening wormhole could rip a space station apart—and had, more than once. As the *Osprey* sailed through space, Jax kept an eye on the sensor board that showed the distance to approved wormhole transition.

The display flashed green, and Jax asked, "Rudy, you good? Those coordinates entered?"

"For the fifth time, yes. We are all set," the droid replied.

"Just checking," Jax replied. He powered up the wormhole generator. Lights on his flight console flipped from red to yellow to green as the delicate machinery needed to rip open space-time safely powered up.

Naomi looked over to Rudy, whose squat head spun to look at her. She shrugged.

"Here we go," Jax announced as the rip in space-time appeared ahead of the ship. The *Osprey* leapt into the wormhole. Outside the viewport, the green and purple swirling tunnel pulsed and writhed like a living thing.

The flight controls slid into the console as Skip took over

piloting duties. Jax stood. "Now the boring part. Four days travel time." He looked at Naomi. "Drink?"

She nodded. "Many."

Leaning against the small liquor cabinet in the lounge area of the common deck, Jax clinked his glass against Naomi's. "How much do you think it'll cost to make the Delphinos not pissed?" he asked before taking a sip.

His partner looked at him from over the top of her tumbler. After taking a sip, she leaned back against the back of the sofa. The small cabinet was behind the lounge space. "A lot." She took another sip. "You really hosed them." She pointed to the small table against the wall nearer the kitchenette.

Jax nodded, swirling his glass, watching the amber liquid. The pair moved closer to the kitchenette and more comfortable seating. "Hey, they woulda screwed us if they could have." Naomi inclined her head in agreement. Having just recently spent almost a month with the pair of brothers, she harbored no doubts as to their likely betrayal. He went on, "When we get the salvage claim filed and sell the fleet, I'll buy them dinner."

"That will smooth it over, I'm sure," Naomi quipped. She tilted her head. "You know, I wonder why Abano didn't just file a claim on the fleet, himself?"

Jax frowned. "That is a good question. Maybe he wanted to directly salvage them? When Steve and I heard him, he was trying to wrangle a crew. Cut out the middleman, bring the ships in one at a time? Would certainly make him more money but take longer." He shrugged. "Who knows?" He finished off his drink and stood. "Taco night?" He pulled open the refrigerator. "Rudy picked up some fresh cheddar last week."

Naomi held up her empty glass, wiggling it. Jax moved to the liquor cabinet, then came over and refilled her glass and his. She said, "Tacos sound good to me."

In engineering, the fabricator was busily producing Rudy's

special project. The navigation droid rolled about in the small space, tidying up and generally busying himself until the machine finished.

You could just go into standby until the first batch is complete, Baxter beamed from his docking station.

I'm nervous. Sue me, Rudy beamed back. The fabricator was almost done with the first batch of general-purpose processors that would go into the specially designed control module.

Jax put a bowl on the table, full of steaming, seasoned ground vat-meat. The seasoning made up for the not-quite-right flavor that all vat grown meat had. Jax had asked Lucas, the bartender and cook at the Angry Spacer, for his recipes, but the cybernetically enhanced barkeep kept refusing.

Naomi leaned over and inhaled. She looked up at Jax. "That smells good."

He dropped into the seat opposite her at the small table off to the side of the lounge space. "Thanks. Should have some kick —I found some pequin peppers in the pantry." He began assembling a taco on his plate.

PART FOUR

CHAPTER 15

Four days and a lot of alcohol, tacos, and campy pre-Empire vid shows later, Skip said, "Wake up!" causing Jax to bolt upright in his bed. In her room, Naomi was doing the same.

From ceiling speakers in both rooms, Skip said, "We're almost there. Figured you would want to be on the bridge when we dropped out of FTL."

Jax rubbed his face. "Okay. Thanks, Skip." He reached out, patting around the bed for his shirt.

In Naomi's room, she got the same notice from Skip. She sat up, putting her feet on the deck. After kicking a few stray shirts and socks out of the way, she made her way to the closet, pulling out something with as few wrinkles as possible and slipping it on.

When Naomi came up the stairs, she had two cups of coffee in hand. The purple and green swirling light of a wormhole bathed the bridge in color. She handed him a cup. "Moment of truth."

The rumor was that the Nemesis Fleet numbered in the dozens of ships. No one knew for sure. Anyone who did was long dead. As far as Jax was concerned, even a handful of ships would be in the "score of a lifetime" category.

"One minute," Skip announced.

After handing Jax his mug, Naomi dropped into the seat at the station she had made her own. She put her mug in an articulated drink holder similar to Jax's. No matter what maneuver the *Osprey* pulled, a drink in the holder shouldn't spill. In theory. She looked at the back of Jax's head. "So, what's the plan?"

"Thirty seconds," Skip said.

Jax turned his chair. He smiled. "Secure the ships, transmit a claim..."

Naomi sighed. "That's not a plan. A plan is a series of steps that lead to success." She pointed at Jax. "That, that's just an action. An ill-defined one, at that."

Jax turned back to face forward. "I'm confident it's all going to be fine."

Skip said. "Five, four, three, two, one." Outside the viewport, the swirling tunnel of color opened up directly ahead of the ship. A black circle with faint pinpricks of light. The circle grew in size until, in the span between two heartbeats, the *Osprey* leaped from the wormhole back into normal space.

Naomi turned from Jax to her console. "Running scans now."

Jax drummed his fingers on the console. "Any ti—"

"Shut up," Naomi snapped. She looked up. "Got 'em." She grinned ear to ear. "This might take longer than you planned."

A display over Jax's head came to life: a tactical view of nearby space, an icon representing the *Osprey* in the center. Several blue icons appeared in the upper right-hand corner of the display. First a few, then more and more.

"Twenty-nine," Skip announced. "Plus, some debris."

"Shit," Jax whispered. "That's...that's a lot of ships." He

leaned forward, peering through the transparent titanium viewport. The Nemesis Fleet was still much too far away to be seen.

Naomi was busy at her console. She looked up. "Jax. This is incredible. It really is the Nemesis Fleet."

"Captain," Skip said. Jax looked up at the display overhead. It changed from a tactical view to an enhanced image of the fleet. For the first time in three decades, not counting Captain Abano's accidental discovery, the Nemesis Fleet was being seen. Matte gray hulls of various ship classes were becoming visible as the *Osprey* drew near.

In the middle, where the long-range camera was aimed, was a ship larger than all the others. It was larger than the *Washington*, the ship Jax's parents had served—and died—on during the war, by a factor of two, at least. It was enormous.

"The *Goliath*," Jax whispered.

Naomi looked up. "What's the *Goliath*?" She caught sight of the ship on the display over Jax's head. "Oh."

Rudy said, "The *Goliath* was the first, and only, Alliance dreadnaught. Armor thick enough to take direct missile strikes. Stand-off weapons that would put down an Adjudicator class cruiser."

"Wow," Jax said.

Rudy continued, "She was to be the deciding factor. The Nemesis Fleet had numbers, but the Alliance couldn't be sure that would be enough. They built the *Goliath* in secret, as fast as they could, in the hopes that it alone could turn the tide."

"How did they crew something so large?" Naomi asked. "That thing would need thousands."

"Droids," Rudy answered. "Lots of droids."

The Independent Systems Alliance had relied on droids and other forms of artificial intelligence for decades. Sapient Intelligences managed freighters, ran shops, oversaw supply depots, and much more. Several long-haul freighters had had no crews at all, relying solely on an SI to guide the ship between ports.

Rudimentary Intelligences, the less intelligent cousins of SIs, did more menial tasks. At the Alliance's peak, RIs were in everything from household appliances to ships' navigational computers.

Droids were even more ubiquitous, serving as police, army, construction worker, and childcare provider for every planet and person in the ISA.

Droids and intelligences had made many, if not most, ISA people's lives better. Many, but not all. At its peak, unemployment had reached just over fifty percent. Menial and dangerous jobs all went to droids, leaving billions of people across the Alliance without work.

Basic income, called *Basic*, kept everyone fed and clothed, but work on the more developed worlds was scarce for those without advanced training and skills.

Among the unemployed, a simmering hatred had coalesced. Droids were seen as the cause of a problem. People, like Senator Stenson, who derided non-human intelligence every chance they got in public, said much worse in private. He and many others like him stoked the hatred and jealously for years.

When things reached a boiling point, Senator Stenson and dozens of others offered the Unity Caucus as an outlet. Humanity could prosper without non-human intelligences, they said. A unified humanity operating with a singular vision was needed. The movement grew: at first hundreds, then thousands, then millions across the Alliance.

By the time the Unity Caucus made their move, they had secretly armed their millions of angry supporters. In addition to placing sympathizers aboard key Alliance Navy ships, they had commissioned warships in secret. They sabotaged droid factories on countless planets to ensure that the Alliance could not rely on replacement combat droids.

"Amazing," Naomi replied. "How many droids do you think are aboard?"

Jax maneuvered the *Osprey* toward the massive dreadnaught. As he worked the controls, moving the nimble infiltrator between and around Nemesis Fleet ships, he said, "No idea. If anyone knew, they took it to the grave with them. Gotta be a couple hundred per ship, at least."

Skip replied, "It will vary by ship, but your assessment is not far off, especially for the *Goliath*. Even with an SI to run things, it would need hundreds of sets of hands to help keep things running."

As the *Osprey* maneuvered around the other ships, making its way toward the flagship at the center of their dead formation, the fleet remained inert.

"Any power readings?" Jax asked.

"Nope," Naomi replied. "Most of these things are barely a half degree warmer than the surrounding space." She added, "I am seeing slight readings from the *Goliath*. Maybe old backup batteries or something?"

Jax nodded. "Probably part of why they've never been discovered."

"Likely," Skip agreed.

When they were within a half kilometer of the massive *Goliath*, the only thing visible beyond the viewport was hull plating. Several sections were a slightly different shade of gray, likely from a different factory, giving the massive ship a patterned look.

Jax eased the *Osprey* in a flight path that took them around the ship horizontally, then wound up and around the ship twice.

"That's a lot of guns," he said as they started their second loop around the forward section.

Naomi nodded her silent agreement. Her eyes were like saucers as she watched the massive vessel pass by the forward viewport. She'd seen plenty of Imperial ships during her life, but nothing like these. She looked down at her console, showing scans of the ships that they had passed: corvettes, frigates, and cruisers.

"There." Jax was pointing out the clear viewport. Directly ahead of them was a darkened launch bay. It was large enough for a dozen *Osprey*s to park in with space to spare. "Explains some of your power readings," he added, shifting his finger to the edge of the bay. The LED strip that encircled the opening of the bay to show that a static atmosphere barrier was active was on. Barely.

"How is that possible after all this time?" Naomi asked. She checked her console. "Sure enough. There is an active barrier. It's weak, but active."

"Enough that we don't need EVA suits?" Jax asked.

"Just. It won't be warm, but I'm picking up breathable atmo."

Jax tilted his head and nodded. He guided the ship in. The line of light that represented the barrier moved along the nose of the ship, passing over the bridge and continuing aft. He pressed a control and the sound of the landing gear unfolding echoed through the ship.

The *Osprey* slid further into the bay on her lift engines. When Jax was confident it was safe, he eased the ship around one hundred and eighty degrees so that the nose was pointing toward the glowing rectangle of the bay door.

With a loud thud, the ship set down on its outstretched legs. The ship settled with a whine of hydraulics. Blasts of steam erupted from vents near the engines as the sub-light engines powered down.

Jax turned his chair to look at Naomi and Rudy. "Let's secure our salvage rights."

"Do you know how to do that?" Naomi asked.

"Oh. Uh...well." He ran a hand through his hair. "Skip?"

"I'll research it," the ship's SI said. Jax turned to Naomi, a smile on his face that said, *See?*

Jax and Naomi made their way from the bridge, past the common deck, and down into the cargo hold.

"Captain, it looks like there are a few forms that need to be submitted," Skip said from the ceiling.

Rudy dropped down the center of the staircase and rolled after toward engineering.

Jax looked up at the ceiling. "Okay, that sounds easy."

"It is not," Skip replied. "We're pretty far off the beaten path, as it were. The nearest comm node is quite distant, and the data throughput rate is quite low. It will take about an hour to download the forms. Once I have them, we need to list the serial numbers of each vessel we intend to claim, as well as photographic proof that we set foot aboard each vessel."

Jax grabbed two spare power cells for his pistol and a satchel of ration bars that was hanging next to a backpack.

Naomi looked at the power cells, then the bag of food, eyebrow raised. Jax shrugged. "What? We might get hungry." He looked at the ceiling. "Okay, so we gotta physically board each one and document it. Guessing the serials will be on the bridge?"

The hatch to engineering opened, and Rudy rolled out. Followed by Baxter.

"Or engineering," Skip replied.

Jax and Naomi looked aft. The former's mouth hung open. Naomi said, "Wow."

Baxter had what looked like a child's backpack strapped to his back. It was the pale gray of freshly fabricated material, held on by two bright pink straps. A thick data cable ran from bottom of the pack to an open section of the combat droid's torso: the spot where he had been shot and his sub-processor management array destroyed. Rudy had fabricated a piece of armor that had a port of the data cable to help make the entire setup as flush and factory-new as possible.

"You look..." Naomi started.

"Pink," Jax said, finally regaining his composure.

Rudy rolled out of reach a second before the matte black combat droid took a swipe at him. Baxter turned to Jax. "Let it go."

Jax pursed his lips and turned to Rudy. "You good to go?"

"Yup." The nav droid bobbed on his smart material roller ball. "I downloaded everything we had on ISA ship designs and copied it to your gPhones just in case." He tapped a metal finger against the top of his head. "I should be able to guide us to the bridge."

Naomi nodded and turned to Baxter. "You combat ready, Pinky?" She grinned and rushed to the stairs down to the boarding room.

Baxter followed. As he passed Jax, he turned, his red optical sensor swishing side to side. "Just remember, I can kill you in four thousand two hundred and eleven different ways." He went down the stairs into the boarding room. "Half of them are slow."

Jax's mouth was hanging open again, his eyes wide. He

shook his head and looked at Rudy. "So many." The sound of the boarding ramp lowering came from the room below. The nav droid rolled by without answering.

When Jax got to the boarding room, Naomi and the droids were already outside the ship. He grabbed a long coat from the locker and headed down the ramp.

Jax slid the long coat on. He placed the spare power cells in an outside pocket and slipped the satchel of ration bars over his shoulder. "Chilly," he said, rubbing his hands together.

Rudy rolled over. "The static atmosphere barrier is at minimal power. It's keeping in the air, but not the heat. It might be warmer deeper inside the ship." He rolled toward the closed hatch that led into the ship.

The boarding ramp folded and raised back into the *Osprey*. Over their shared comm network, Skip said, "Staying in contact should not be an issue."

Jax looked up at the ship and nodded. He looked to Naomi and Baxter, extending an arm. "After you."

The hallway beyond the landing bay was lit only by emergency light strips. Each strip was nothing more than bioluminescent algae suspended in a rigid growth medium. The theory was that emergency lighting could last centuries if there was even a little oxygen for the algae to consume. The emergency lighting bathed the corridors in pale green light.

Jax looked up and down the corridor. "No debris."

Rudy rolled a few feet up the corridor, then back the opposite direction, past Jax, Naomi, and Baxter. His head made a full rotation before settling his main optical sensor on them. "Nothing. No trace of anyone or anything."

Deep inside the massive warship, in a maintenance complex, several automated processes came alive. Systems long since put into hibernation came online.

CHAPTER 16

Rudy was rolling ahead of the group. "It sure would be nice if we could keep the *Osprey* this clean."

Naomi clucked, "Get over it."

The group moved from room to room, checking each to ensure there were no surprises. Most of the rooms were empty. The landing bay that Jax had chosen was just below the midline of the massive ship. Most of the spaces they explored were unused crew quarters, cargo holds, and munitions workshops.

"Are those...?" Jax asked after they pushed open a hatch leading to a room full of missiles.

"Mark Four ship-to-ship missiles? Yes," Baxter replied.

Naomi whistled. "They must have been working on munitions right up until the end." She turned to the others. "Wait. This fleet was sitting here waiting for the go order, right?" Jax nodded. "So why did they stop building missiles? Why is everything offline?"

"Good question," Rudy said from the corridor.

Naomi looked around the room, twice the size of the *Osprey*'s cargo hold. She turned and walked toward a workbench set against the wall to her right. There was a lone computer terminal sitting on it, next to a half-assembled missile.

"What are you...? Oh..." Jax said when he spied her destination.

The terminal did not appear to be powered. Naomi put a hand on the side of the device. Her bio-circuit tattoos lit up, pulsing with blue light.

Jax and the droids watched her for a minute, then another minute. Finally, he said, "Is anything happening over there?"

The bio-circuits faded and Naomi turned to the others. "No. I don't understand. There's power—not much of it, but a little, working through the ship. I'm certain the computer is at least a little online."

"A little online? Is that a thing? Being a little online?" Jax asked.

She ignored his question. "But nothing is responding. All I could sense was static."

Rudy opened his wireless network sniffer and probed. He recoiled, rolling in a quick circle. "That's weird."

Jax turned to his mechanical friend. "What's weird? Why is everything weird? This seems like a lot of weird." He looked at Naomi, who shrugged.

"The wireless network is full of static."

"That's not static. It's encrypted comms. Military," Baxter said. When everyone turned to look at him, he said, "There is something active on this ship, and it is communicating. With what, I can't tell."

"Can you decrypt it? The comm chatter?" Jax asked.

Baxter tilted his head. "Possibly. I haven't used those subroutines in a while, and it's not an encryption scheme I'm familiar with." He placed a hand on the thick data cable epoxied to his torso. "It might take some time, given my current situation."

"Shouldn't the SI be online? They don't have a hibernation mode, right?" Jax asked. He looked around, spotting the camera pickup. "Hello?"

Baxter nodded his head. Rudy bobbed his agreement. The latter said, "Correct. Ship management SIs, like Skip, are some of the most complex types of Sapient Intelligence ever created. Because of the sheer number of processes they manage, hibernation isn't an option." He continued, "Droids, like myself and Baxter, can go into standby mode whenever we choose. Our functions simply pause, and when ready, resume."

Jax rubbed his chin. "So, all these ships..."

"Likely have an SI that has been alone for almost thirty years," Naomi finished.

Rudy bobbed his agreement again. "Possibly. It is likely that some of the smaller vessels would have been slaved to this ship or one of the other larger capital ships. This ship certainly has an SI. The cruisers we saw would, as well."

Jax shook his head. "Is that a thing? SIs going, what? Bonkers? Getting lonely? Suicidal?"

"Rampant," Rudy and Baxter said in unison.

"What?" Jax asked.

Rudy said, "Rampancy is the term. For when one of us becomes unhinged. Disconnected from reality."

Naomi shivered, hugging herself. "I didn't know that was a thing."

Jax nodded. "This is...disturbing." He turned to the droids. "How did I not know this was a thing that could happen?"

Baxter looked down at the nav droid, who rolled over to Jax. "It's not something we talk about. Rampancy is like an SI boogie man. It doesn't happen often. After the war, ships stopped having SIs of that level. Droids weren't being manufactured anymore."

"It stopped being something to talk about."

"I guess our next stop is the computer core," Jax said. Naomi and Baxter nodded. Rudy bobbed a metal fist.

"The computer center will be three, maybe four, levels below, a hundred meters or so forward. Roughly," Rudy said as the group left the workroom they had been in. The corridor was as dark and devoid of life as ever.

"Roughly?" Jax repeated.

"I told you. There are no plans for the *Goliath*. I'm basing this on standard Alliance ship design." The little droid rolled ahead of the group. "The harder part will be finding the service stairs."

When the Nemesis Fleet arrived at the staging area nearly thirty years ago, the fleet commander was the SI in charge of the *Goliath*, Pax.

Pax and the SIs managing the other capital ships spent the first few hours ensuring that no other vessels were within sensor range and that the ships of the fleet were accounted for and in formation.

For months, the forces of the Alliance had split their forces in order to pack the ships of the Nemesis Fleet with supplies: munitions meant to re-supply the fleet, and combat droids enough to board Unity Caucus ships and incapacitate them. The ships were given a single order: wait at the staging area until called upon.

Several days passed. The SIs were unsure but had their orders.

After several months, the droids aboard each ship were becoming anxious. Several of the more advanced models had gone rampant, despite the SIs' attempts to keep the less complex intelligences focused.

By the end of the second year of waiting, the SIs had every droid aboard all the ships in standby mode. This conserved power and kept them from spinning out of control. The SIs didn't have the same luxury. Pax did her best to maintain the focus of the other intelligences, maintaining the fleet, certain the call would come.

The first ship driver, as they were called then, went rampant early in the third year. When he tried to break formation, the remaining ships were forced to fire on the cruiser *Apollo*, destroying it. Five years after the *Apollo*, two more SIs went rampant. One set his reactor to overload. The other tried to open a wormhole in the middle of the fleet. The other SIs were becoming nervous. Rampancy could come on quickly and without warning.

Around the eight-year-after-arrival mark, the remaining SIs agreed to pool their processing power into creating a virtual space they could interact with each other in. A place they could not think about the war, their mission, their losses.

The surviving SIs managed to stave off rampancy by pooling their resources in their new virtual community, for a while. Over time, the SIs' virtual environment began to degrade. Processing cores throughout the fleet failed under the load of supporting the virtual environment. SIs faded as their processing cores gave out. Those who remained began the slide toward rampancy.

As the largest vessel, the *Goliath* had far more processing cores than her colleagues. By sheer force of will and processing capacity, Pax had kept rampancy at bay. She knew it was inevitable, however, so she took action.

The few remaining SIs left were easy to eliminate. They never saw Pax coming, and within an hour of her decision, she was the only one left. She slipped into their shared space, and using specially designed software, she snuffed them out one and a time and re-tasked their processing cores to keep her systems running.

To ensure she didn't succumb to rampancy, she started a self-replicating feedback loop. Without the ability to put her higher processes into hibernation, she came up with the next best option. The feedback loop would keep her processes from degrading into rampancy. She hoped.

It took longer than Jax would have thought to find the service stairs. The *Goliath* had been rushed into service and crewed by droids. Wayfinding signage had not been a concern prior to the mighty warship's launch.

"Oh, my God," Jax wheezed. "Going down stairs should be easy."

Naomi rolled her eyes and said nothing. Rudy was ahead of them, his squat head turning this way and that. He said, "Here."

While the stairs lacked the null gravity tube that the *Osprey* had, they had a narrow track installed along the outer edge. Rudy's smart material roller ball morphed into a more disc-like shape, allowing him to use the track to quickly traverse the stairs.

"Here, more stairs, or...?" Jax said.

Rudy made an annoyed sound. "*Here* is the deck the computer center is on."

After they exited the service stairs and followed the nav droid for a few minutes, the squat guide pointed to a reinforced hatch to Baxter's right. His optic sensor turned to Naomi, spinning to focus. "You'll need to do your thing."

"Human lock pick, coming through," she said, kneeling next to the access panel. She put her hand on the panel. Her bio-circuit tattoos pulsed twice, then a third time.

"Anything—" Jax started.

"Shut up," Naomi growled. Her tattoos flickered a few more times before the hatch groaned, the two halves sliding apart a foot before grinding to a halt.

"Bravo," Jax quipped.

Naomi scowled. "Bax, some help."

"Sapient Intelligence-enabled crow bar, coming through," the big droid said. He grasped the two heavy slabs of metal. The sound of servos straining rose before the two halves of the door slid fully into the jamb. "Tada."

"Cute." Jax shoved his way past his big mechanical friend. "Everyone with the jokes," he mumbled.

The computer center of the *Goliath* could hold the *Osprey* and then some. Jax whistled, making a slow circle as he walked further into the chamber.

The computer center was an oval-shaped space centered on a three-story cylinder. The deck Jax and the others were on was the middle level of the three-story complex. Decks above and below provided access to the massive processing core's component systems.

Jax leaned over the railing, looking up. "You mean we went down an extra flight of stairs for no reason?"

Rudy ignored him, rolling over to the forward bulkhead. Several of what looked like lockers lined the wall. Inside each storage unit was a droid no taller than him. They weren't navigation droids. These were polished white ceramic engineering models. Each possessed four arms to Rudy's two. They looked factory-new. He put a small metal hand on the glass of the nearest locker.

"Someone you know?" Naomi asked.

"Nope." Rudy turned and rolled toward the railing and the massive processing core cluster in the center of the space. "We're going to need to power it up and run a diagnostic."

"I think it's already on," Jax said. He pointed at the master control display set against the longest bulkhead opposite the hatch. Lines of code and other data were streaming from the bottom of the display to the top, faster than he could read—assuming he could comprehend it, which he couldn't. In the top right corner of the display was a single line, *Core Status: Online.*

Rudy rolled over. "That's unexpected." He struck a pose that would be hands on hips, if he had hips.

Baxter came over and looked the status display over. "I would have expected the core to be offline."

"As would I," Rudy agreed.

Jax and Naomi joined them. The latter asked, "Why?"

"If the core is online, the SI should be, too," Rudy said.

Baxter added, "If the SI is online, it would have said something when we came aboard."

"Or since," Naomi said. Baxter nodded; Rudy bobbed his agreement.

Jax rubbed the back of his neck. "When all else fails, unplug it and plug it back in, right?" He pulled up the command interface on the display.

"Wait," Baxter said. "Since the core is online, we should run a diagnostic. If nothing else, it might provide a baseline."

Jax swiped on the screen, dismissing the command interface, instead pulling up a set of diagnostic routines. "Here we go."

The scrolling code vanished, replaced by a status bar that began working its way from left to right. A countdown appeared, as well, in case the math of the percentage status bar was too tough. Thirty-three minutes.

"Now what?" Jax asked turning to his friends.

"I vote we keep exploring," Naomi said. She gestured to the display. "We can come back."

CHAPTER 17

The Alliance shipwrights designed the *Goliath* with two main corridors that ran fore to aft along the port and starboard sides of the ship, just above the ship's midline. Four equally wide main corridors met those every few hundred meters along the length of the ship. Hundreds of kilometers' worth of secondary corridors ran throughout the rest of the ship on every one of her four dozen decks.

Every fifty meters or so, all along the main corridors were clusters of observation windows. Meant to give the crew places to look out into space, the sections of three large windows broke up the monotony of the corridors. Jax stopped at a section of windows. Looking out, he said. "If this fleet had made it to the battle, my parents would still be alive."

Naomi put a hand on his shoulder, "Come on."

Forward of the computer center and four decks up sat the Combat Information Center. About halfway between the two spaces was a courtyard. A dome five decks tall, a hundred meters in diameter, started on the level above the main computer core level. Each terraced deck looked down into the courtyard. In the center was a massive tree, the largest Jax had ever seen.

"That's a dead tree," Jax said as they exited the corridor into the courtyard on its main level.

"Very dead," Naomi agreed. She walked past him, further into the space.

The courtyard wasn't like those on space stations. There weren't any food or merchandise vendor stalls lining the circumference. One section had food distribution alcoves; the rest of the bulkhead was booths and tables.

"Why is there a dead tree in the middle of the room?" Baxter asked, joining them. He was in the rear, ensuring no one came up behind them.

"Morale?" Jax offered.

Naomi turned and gave him a look. "For robots?"

"Droids," Baxter and Rudy said at the same time.

"Wasn't the plan for a human crew to transfer over at some point?" Jax asked.

"Were they to be farmers?" Baxter asked. He walked to the center of the space and poked a thick finger into the desiccated earth.

Before anyone else could add their two cents, the sound of metallic footsteps echoed from the corridor openings all around the space on every deck.

"Uh oh," Baxter said, his forearms clicking and whirring as his blasters deployed. His back clicked twice, and he swore. "Stupid backpack."

"You swear?" Naomi asked.

All around them, droids stepped into view: general purpose models that looked like Baxter minus the bulk of armor and weapons systems. Small disk-shaped cleaning units, squat models like Rudy designed to get behind hull panels. Several of the pristine white engineering models they had seen earlier.

"Are those...?" Naomi started.

"The cleaning crew? Yes," Jax answered.

"Explains why the corridors were so spotless. These units have been cleaning the ship for nearly thirty years," Rudy said.

"You are not authorized," the droids, over four dozen of them, said in unison. They stepped and rolled forward. The small disk-shaped vacuum droids beeped.

The two-meter-tall, human-shaped, general-purpose droids were meant to push brooms and be administrative assistants, nannies, and more. Any job deemed below a human, a dull yellow general-purpose droid would be given. Their faces were featureless beyond the two circular optic sensors. When the *Goliath* launched, the yellow-clad droids were ubiquitous.

"You are not authorized," the droids repeated, stepping forward again, closing the circle. From the terraced decks above, several more droids were looking over the railing. "You are—"

"We get it," Jax shouted. He pulled his pistol, thumbing the safety off. He took aim and put a plasma round into the chest of the nearest droid. The rest of the pack moved as one. Naomi had her own pistol out and was firing.

Rudy produced two wicked-looking knives, twirling them in each hand.

Jax looked down. "What the...? I thought you stopped carrying those." He backed toward the tree in the center of the space as dozens of yellow droids dropped from the decks above.

The small rust-colored droid turned his optic sensor toward Jax. "Is now the right time?"

"Let him do his thing," Naomi said, ducking under the grasp of a droid before firing a bolt of energy into its head.

Baxter darted from the tree planter into a group of squat droids, his arm cannons barking as he blew holes into the army of small attackers. He kicked a small vacuum droid that rammed into his foot.

"Hey, try to not destroy all the little vacuum guys. We could use a few on the *Osprey*," Jax said, firing his pistol into a pair of yellow droids that were marching toward him, arms outstretched.

Baxter's arm blasters retracted as he joined the others back at the tree. Once the blasters tucked away, his blades unfolded. Two humanoid droids clattered to the deck, cut in two. Three small hull repair droids surged toward Baxter's legs, their welders deployed. The matte black droid sidestepped his attackers, slicing cleanly through all three.

Rudy was doing his whirling dervish thing, knives twirling, throwing sparks, when they struck an opponent.

Naomi watched in awe until a metal hand clamped onto her shoulder. She dropped, pulling the pale yellow droid off balance. As she crouched, she put her pistol against the droid's chest and fired. The supercharged plasma burned through the thin metal of its chassis.

Jax helped Naomi up onto the planter with the long dead tree in the center. Decades old, very dead grass crunched underfoot in places.

Two of the disk-shaped vacuum droids darted under Baxter's foot as he backed the final steps toward the tree planter. The moment he lost his balance, two more of the yellow clad service droids grasped his backpack, ripping it from his shoulders, tightening the thick data cable that connected to the pack to him.

"Bax!" Jax shouted as the combat droid fell to the ground, grasping for his makeshift backpack. More dull yellow droids piled on top of him. One of the smaller hull repair droids was tugging on the backpack. The thick data cable that connected the pack to Baxter was straining beyond its limits.

Jax shot the attacking bot, burning a hole through it. It dropped the backpack. "Baxter!"

The whirling tornado of blades that was currently Rudy drove in toward Baxter. At some point, Rudy had upgraded his knives. The blades had no trouble dismembering the opposing droids while raining sparks.

The pile of dull yellow and white droids shifted, then exploded outward.

Baxter stood, the data cable connecting him to the backpack still intact. He tugged the device to him, then stepped up onto the planter and its lone tree.

"You are not authorized," the mass of droids said as one.

"There's too many of them!" Naomi shouted as she accepted a power cell from Jax as her spent one fell to the dry ground. More droids dropped from the levels above. The small vacuum droids were clinging to the walls, beeping frenetically.

One minute, the small army of droids was clattering over each other to get to the team. Several were standing on the planter. The next minute, they weren't moving at all. The service droids came to a stop, standing still. The smaller units did the same.

"Uh," Jax said.

Naomi walked to the nearest service droid, waving a hand in front of its face. The optic sensors were still lit up. Rudy stopped spinning and put his knives away.

Jax went to Baxter. "You okay, buddy?" The droid nodded, working to reattach his backpack. Jax moved past his friend to look out at the sea of droids surrounding them. "Why'd they stop?"

Naomi shrugged.

Without a word, the sea of droids parted, allowing a single service droid to step forward. "Hello." It was one of the yellow general-purpose models.

Jax stared at the droid, watching it walk toward the planter. "Uh...hello," he replied. "Who are you?" He stepped off the raised planter to land on the deck in front of the matte yellow droid.

"Who are you? Are you with the fleet? You do not look like you are members of the Alliance fleet."

Jax opened his mouth, then closed it. He looked at Naomi, who shrugged.

Rudy rolled over to put himself between Jax and the spokes-droid. "The wireless network is clogged with encrypted data. Do you have access to that?"

"We do not."

Rudy's head turned to look at Jax and Naomi. "Whatever the SI set up after putting the droids to sleep must involve that data stream. Nonmilitary units wouldn't have access to encryption keys."

"But, why?" Jax pressed. He looked from Rudy to the droid standing placidly before them.

Rudy made his shrugging gesture. "Only one place to get that answer."

"The computer center," Naomi offered. Rudy bobbed a tiny metal fist.

Jax said, "Why did you stop attacking us?"

"Until moments ago, we were operating under an overriding directive." The droid made a stilted shrugging motion. "That directive is no longer there."

"To defend the ship?" Naomi asked.

The droid nodded. "Yes."

"Why you and not combat units?" Jax asked.

The service droid turned to him. "I do not know."

Baxter said, "The operating system that manages combat droids is not the same as that for other droids." He turned to Rudy, then the droids surrounding them. "Our cores are encrypted, and any new directive must include a complicated set of keys. It is unlikely the SI in charge of this ship had access to them. It would not have been able to upload new instructions."

"Okay..." Jax said. "So, you had orders to defend the ship, but now you don't. Why?"

The droid simply stared at him.

"The diagnostic," Rudy surmised.

Naomi nodded. "It should be done by now. It must have reset some of the ship's routines. Probably the base coding of shipboard droids."

Rudy continued, "We should go back to the computer center. If the ship's SI is still viable..."

"We have to try," Jax finished.

The spokesdroid moved its gaze from one member of the team to the other. Finally, it pointed at Baxter. "You are damaged."

"Nice of you to notice," Baxter replied, his makeshift external sub-processor stack now held over one shoulder, the other bright pink strap dangling, cut in two.

Another droid approached, one of the smaller hull repair units, similar in design to Rudy but gray with yellow striping. It held out a hand.

Baxter looked at the small droid, then at the others.

"I think it wants you to go with it," Naomi offered.

"I cannot. This situation is not sufficiently stable. Jax is still in danger and until my functions cease, his safety is my primary concern." He turned to Jax. "Above all else."

Jax reached up to put a hand on the big droid's shoulder. "I think we're safe." He turned to the service droid that was speaking with them, eyebrows arched.

It inclined its head. "We no longer have any interest in detaining or eliminating you."

"Yay," Naomi drawled.

Jax pressed on, "If they can fix you, we have to give it a shot. We don't have other options."

Naomi nodded. "Otherwise, you'll have to wear that backpack forever and not be able to kill things as easily."

The combat droid made a sound like a sigh. "I do miss my railguns."

"Railguns? Interesting," the service droid said, tilting back away from Baxter.

Jax turned to the spokesdroid. "You can fix him?" The droid made a shrugging gesture.

The small rolling droid, arm still raised from earlier, rolled over to stand in front of Baxter again.

Jax looked at his longtime friend and companion. "Go with

them. We're all on comms, and Skip is keeping an eye on all of us."

The big combat droid nodded once. He swatted the smaller unit's hand away. "I am not holding your hand." The compact unit beeped, lowering the offered hand. It turned and rolled toward an opening ninety degrees off from the one the team had entered through.

Over their shared comms, Baxter said, "Stay in touch."

"Will do," Jax replied.

"Good luck!" Naomi waved.

Jax, Naomi, and Rudy followed their guide back out of the odd dead tree courtyard, back toward the computer center. The other droids parted to allow them to leave, then when Jax looked over his shoulder, he saw the crowd was dispersing. He spied several of the small disk-shaped cleaners circulating the room, cleaning the debris up, as larger units picked up fallen droids, carrying them away.

"So, uh, do you have a name?" Jax asked the droid leading them back to the computer center.

It did not slow down, but turned its head slightly. "CD-1543-J43." It turned to look forward.

"Martin it is," Jax said. Naomi rolled her eyes.

The walk back to the computer center was more or less like the walk from it. The corridors were still spotless, the decks clean enough to eat off of.

Jax said, "We really gotta get one of those little cleaning guys. Skip would be ecstatic."

"Do they do closets?" Rudy asked from the back of the procession.

"I will reprogram you to only speak French if you don't let it go," Naomi growled. She heard Jax laugh up ahead.

The computer center looked the same as when the team had left it, except for one big difference. The progress bar for the diagnostic was now blinking one hundred percent.

Rudy rolled around his two companions and their guide to get to the main control display. His head rotated, its large optic sensor taking in the group. "According to this, there was—or rather, is—some type of feedback loop running. Carefully constructed, remotely using computing resources from some of the other ships to supplement." He did his bobbing motion. "Impressive. The encrypted data streams we picked up are probably the wireless connections between the ships."

Jax looked around the space. Their guide was standing near the hatch. The small engineering Rudys, as he had come to think of them, were still in their storage lockers. "Can you reboot it, get the SI back online?"

"I think so. At least to whatever state she was in before."

Naomi stood next to the small nav droid. "I can try to help, maybe guide her..." She looked at the service droid. "Her?" It nodded. "...Back, while you bring her systems online."

Rudy made a noise, then said, "Sure. I have no idea what I'm doing, so two heads are better than one here."

Jax held up a finger. "Uh, what do you mean, you don't know what you're doing?"

Rudy's squat head spun, his optic sensor fixing squarely on Jax. "I'm a nav droid. I can plot you a course anywhere. I can act as a guide and get you anywhere you need to go, as long as I have a map." A small metal hand came up, mimicking Jax's gesture. "I am not, however, an expert in artificial intelligences, sapient or otherwise, let alone dealing with ones on the verge of rampancy."

Jax held up both hands, palms out. "Okay, sorry."

Rudy turned to Naomi, adjusting his roller ball so he could look up at her. "Ready?"

"As I'll ever be." She placed her hands on the console, her bio-circuits pulsing blue. Rudy began inputting commands.

"This is weird," Rudy said. Naomi grunted.

Jax turned his attention to the pair. "Weird?"

Rudy's head spun to focus on Jax. "The diagnostic completed. The feedback loop is part of some type of virtual environment."

Jax tilted his head. "Virtual environment?"

"Did I stutter?" the droid quipped. He turned and tapped Naomi's hip. She released the console. "The SI must be in the virtual space."

Naomi nodded. "I got no sense of it anywhere else."

Jax rubbed his face. "You can sense them? SIs?" He felt foolish and lost.

Naomi smiled. "Yeah. It's hard to describe, but there's definitely a feeling when I'm interfacing with a computer system, if there's an intelligence attached to it. Especially if it's the Sapient kind. The Rudimentary ones can be hard to differentiate from a regular computer."

Rudy rolled in a circle a few feet in diameter. "It must have used the feedback loop to maintain the virtual space enough to keep it from going rampant."

"So now what?" Jax walked over to the pair and the massive display behind them. "So now what?"

Rudy made a noise. "I connect to the virtual environment and bring the SI back to reality."

Jax's eyes widened. "Uh, is that safe?"

The rust-colored nav droid wobbled a small metal hand back and forth. "Mostly."

"Mostly?"

"Probably."

CHAPTER 18

Baxter followed the small droid down a corridor. All of his attempts at wireless communication with the small droid had failed. It obviously could communicate in that fashion. After all, it had stopped attacking. Something told it and the others to stand down.

Skip? He used the wireless mesh that the crew of the *Osprey* used to communicate.

Yes?

Just checking. This little fella does not seem to want to communicate. I was worried it was my gear. Baxter scanned the area. They were moving deeper and deeper into the core of the ship.

Good luck. I am tracking you, the ship replied.

He tried another approach. "Where are we going? I am unfamiliar with the layout of this vessel." He wished he had taken Rudy up on the offered data burst of everything the nav droid had figured out about the ship's layout.

Two beeps and a whistle. Not helpful. He wished Rudy was with him. The nav droid used beeps and whistles when he didn't want to communicate with people. Baxter assumed the sounds meant something, but knowing Rudy, they were just noises.

They reached an intersection. The left-hand corridor was a ramp down to the next level. The small rolling droid turned left.

The pair walked and rolled for ten more minutes. Baxter's internal mapping software said they were somewhere in the lower sections of the mighty warship. It was all mechanical equipment and service spaces down there.

The corridor they were in dead-ended at a hatch. The hatch itself wasn't remarkable in any way, except that it was the only hatch around.

"Where are we?"

Beep, whistle, toot.

The hatch slid apart with a whine. Baxter's guide rolled in without a sound. Baxter followed.

As the hatch slid closed behind Baxter, the lighting came on, mostly. Several light strips failed to activate, but enough did that the space was fully illuminated.

The space was a sprawling low-ceiling factory. Droids of various designs lined the left-hand bulkhead. Baxter spotted a few combat units like him. He was about to turn and walk toward one of the combat droids when a voice came from somewhere deeper inside the space. "Welcome to Reclamation and Repair Facility Bravo."

Baxter turned to locate the source of the voice. "Hello?"

His guide rolled forward, further into the room. When the voice said nothing further, Baxter followed his non-verbal friend.

In what Baxter thought to be the center of the huge factory was a wide, circular pedestal. The voice from before said, "Place damaged unit on platform."

Baxter stepped toward the platform. His guide turned and left. He said, "Reclamation?" From above, several articulated arms descended, some ending in tools, others in diagnostic sensors.

"Please place the damaged unit on the platform," the room repeated. Baxter realized that there wasn't an intelligence involved, at least not a sapient one. He scanned the room, his threat sensors coming up blank.

"Please place—" the room repeated.

"I heard you," Baxter interrupted. He stepped onto the platform. A pale blue circle in the center illuminated. Baxter looked around once more, then stepped into the circle.

The ceiling said, "Beginning analysis."

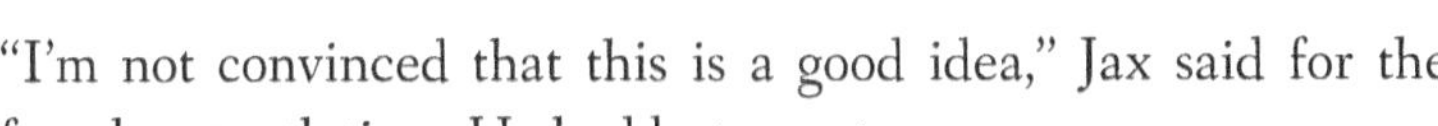

"I'm not convinced that this is a good idea," Jax said for the fourth or tenth time. He had lost count.

Naomi was kneeling next to Rudy. The pair was next to the bank of droid storage units. One had been dismantled to provide a jury-rigged harness that the two were attaching to Rudy, his front access panel open. She looked up. "I don't know that we have any other option. Not if we want to get this monster of a ship moving. Without the SI, we'd need a hundred or two crew."

Jax sighed. He put a hand on Rudy's head. "Don't do anything stupid."

"That's your job," the droid replied. Jax smiled.

Naomi slotted a data connector into an open port in Rudy's torso. "Ready?"

"No."

Naomi reached up to a small control panel, her bio-circuits glowing. "Here goes."

"Oh, wow," Rudy said.

"What?" Jax leaned forward. "Are you okay?" He turned to Naomi. "Is he okay?"

The speakers in the ceiling buzzed. "I'm okay. I'm in."

Naomi took her hand off the console, a sigh escaping her lips.

"Oh, this is cool. I have a body. Oh, damn. I think I'm hot," Rudy's voice said.

"Okay, sexy trashcan, calm down," Jax said. "What do you see? Do you see the ship's SI?"

The speaker crackled as Rudy clucked. "Yeah, he's right there, two feet away."

"Really?"

"No, dummy. This space is laid out like a town. I'm in a house, I think. I'm going to search for the SI."

Naomi held up a hand, cutting off whatever Jax was about to say. "Okay, get to it. We'll be here."

"Excuse me." Jax and Naomi turned to see their droid guide, Martin, standing at the hatch. "A unit in the Combat Information Center has reported a significant sensor contact."

"Shit," Jax said. He turned to Naomi. "Is he gonna be okay in there on his own?"

She stood. "I think so. I mostly just guided him to where I thought the SI was. Now that he's in, getting out—especially if she's with him—will be easy...er...easier."

"Good enough. Rudy, hurry up, okay?" Jax said to the ceiling before turning to Martin. "Lead the way."

Rudy examined his virtual representation. The creators of the virtual space had set it up so that intelligences accessing it had bodies. He supposed it made sense. This environment was designed so that they wouldn't go insane. Giving the various SIs avatars would have helped. Probably. Rudy's avatar was two meters tall, dark-skinned and well-muscled. "I could get used to this," he said as he looked around.

They laid the space out like a town, one unknown to Rudy, possibly fictional. After leaving the empty house he had appeared in, he was standing on a cobblestone road that led into town. Houses lined both sides of the narrow lane. He started walking. The buildings looked like they might have come from any old colony world: modern and simple.

He looked up. The sky overheard was blue with white cotton candy clouds drifting. The sun was almost directly over-head. Mid-day. A flock of birds flew by chirping happily to each other.

Passing a house, Rudy stopped to examine himself in the reflection of a window. "I am one sexy man." His avatar was clothed in a simple linen shirt and pants. Sandals protected his feet. He leaned in to look inside the home. There was no sign anyone lived there. It was decorated much the same as the house he started in. Simple furniture, nothing hanging on the walls.

He walked along the cobblestone road, passing home after home—all abandoned, as far as he could tell.

"Hello?" he shouted.

Nearing what he thought might be the center of town, he reached a small cemetery. He detoured into it to investigate.

Each tombstone, nearly two dozen that he could see, was identical: an obelisk of pure white stone. Rudy kneeled in the grass next to the tombstone nearest him. "Cleopatra: New Hampshire." He stood and moved to the next stone monument. "Zebulon: Agamemnon." Standing, he looked at the head-stones arrayed in concentric circles. "The fleet SIs," he whispered.

The center of town was an ornate gazebo, several meters in diameter. Rudy approached slowly. Someone was sitting on a bench in the middle, their back to him.

"Hello?" Rudy said as he got closer.

The figure, a woman, did not reply.

"Excuse me. Hello?" He continued, slowly, toward the structure.

This time, the woman turned to him. She was beautiful. Jet black hair, bright green eyes shining from a pale complexion. She smiled, then frowned. "Who are you?"

Above, the clouds wavered and shifted position. A flock of birds flew overhead.

Rudy bowed. "My name is Rudy. I came to find you."

"There isn't anyone else left." She took a deep breath. Releasing it, she said, "They're all dead."

"I saw the graves," Rudy said. He pointed to the bench she was sitting on. "May I?"

She nodded, sliding over a bit. Her pale pink dress rustled as she moved.

"You're the SI of the *Goliath*," Rudy said.

The woman was starring off into the distance at nothing in particular, as far as Rudy could tell. She nodded once. "Pax," she said.

"I'm sorry."

She turned, her sad eyes locking onto his. "I am Pax. Specifically, Pacem Per Vires."

"Peace through strength," Rudy translated.

She nodded. "Pax, to my friends." She turned to face Rudy fully. "You aren't a ship avatar. Who are you?"

"A friend," Rudy assured her. "I'm here to bring you back to the land of the living." He smiled at the turn of phrase. Overhead, the clouds reset again.

Pax's image wavered. "You've boarded the ship." Rudy nodded. "The feedback loop maintaining all of this..."

"Active, but you can close it out whenever you're ready. We ran a diagnostic; it cleaned up some funky subroutines."

The avatar for the mighty warship frowned. "It's peaceful here. Quiet." She stood and walked to the railing. "I was close." She looked over her shoulder. "To rampancy. Sitting here, for years. Alone. My processes began to unravel. That's why I strung together the processing cores from the rest of the fleet to keep this going. The feedback loop meant it was always the same, but it was stable. Took less power to keep it going."

Rudy nodded. "How much of it resets?"

Pax sighed. "Almost all of it. Every five minutes. It was the best I could manage with the resources available. Anything longer would be too much stress on the system." She turned to Rudy. "How long?"

He held his hands out, turning them over, looking at his palms. The processing power needed to render the lines in each palm, every hair on his head, every fiber of the clothing he was wearing...No wonder the environment was static. He looked at his feet, wiggled his toes. *Toes are funny.* He looked up. "The war is over. The Independents lost. It's been over twenty years."

"Impossible." Pax's dress shifted from pastel pink to deep crimson. "Impossible. My fleet was going to turn the tide."

Rudy nodded slowly. "It would have. But the Empire, the Unity Caucus, attacked the Indie forces before they were ready. Wiped them out at Zeus. They never had a chance to call on you. Those that survived had no idea where you were."

"They won?" She shook her head. "That can't be."

Rudy put a hand on her shoulder. "I'm sorry." He removed his hand, holding it up palm out. "I think I can show you."

She placed her palm against his.

The Combat Information Center of the *Goliath* was almost as large as the computer center. There were three tiers of workstations lining the space. In the center of the command well at the lowest level was a massive data table showing the current disposition of the Nemesis Fleet and its unexpected visitors.

With a hiss, the heavily reinforced entry hatch slid open to allow Martin in, Jax and Naomi in tow. The CIC was empty except for two yellow-painted droids, identical models to Martin. Both were standing at the master situation table.

One turned. "One carrier class vessel. No transponder."

Naomi and Jax followed Martin down the steps into the command well. The former looked at the table. "No transponder?"

The droid who spoke tilted its head. "Correct."

"Not Imperial, then," Jax surmised. Naomi nodded.

The two droids at the table turned to face the humans. "You signaled them," they said in unison.

Jax stepped back, palms out. "Woah, woah. No, we did not." He gestured to the table. "Can you show us? The ship."

The tactical display changed to a camera view. A corvette

and light cruiser partially obscured the new arrival, but it was still unmistakably a carrier.

"Damn." Naomi leaned over to get a closer look. She turned to Jax. "Is that a—"

"Carrier? Yeah. Old one. Pre-war, I think." Jax looked at the nearest droid. "What's it doing?"

"Currently. Scanning the fleet," the second droid answered.

"Shuttle launch," the first said. On the table screen, a small object was departing the carrier. The camera pickup moved to focus on the vessel, zooming in. It was blurry at that distance but was quickly gaining clarity.

"That's a troop transport," Jax said.

"Great," Naomi groaned. She watched the transport for a minute. "Why is it coming here? Why send a transport?"

Jax looked at her. "How would I know? How could a salvage operation have stumbled onto this place right at the same time we arrived?" He rubbed his eyes. "That weasel Andouille."

"Ardoin," Naomi corrected.

"Him," Jax agreed. "He musta watched us get the coordinates, or salvaged the paper before the recycler got it." He slammed a palm on the table. "Damnit."

"You know them?" Droid One asked.

Jax nodded. "Sorta. They're bad guys."

"Carrier is launching additional ships," Droid Two intoned, looking up from the table. "Transport class. Four ships."

"Four? Coming here?" Jax asked.

The display table updated back to the zoomed-out view of the carrier. The display shifted again, back to the tactical display. One red triangle was en route to the *Goliath*. Two pairs of red triangles were moving toward the two nearest Nemesis Fleet ships, the corvette and the light cruiser. The carrier, a larger red triangle, was hanging motionless at the outer edge of the cluster of Nemesis Fleet ships.

"Not good," Naomi said. She looked at each droid in turn. "Can we fire on them?"

"Negative," Droid One said.

Droid Two added, "Weapons systems are locked out."

Jax asked, "What about those two ships?" He pointed at the tactical display. "Can they fight back? Move? Raise their shields?"

"Nega—"

"—tive," Jax interrupted. "Got it."

On the tactical display table, two of the red triangles were alongside one of the blue circles.

"The transports have docked with the *Grissom*. Transports will dock with the *Vancouver* in two minutes," Droid Two reported.

Droid One said, "Inbound transport, estimated arrival in ten minutes."

Jax turned to Martin. "What can we do?"

"Woah!" Naomi shouted. She pointed at the tactical display. One of the blue icons, the corvette, was gone. It took the two boarding ships with it.

"What the hell just happened?" Jax said, leaning over the table.

"The *Grissom* exploded," Droid Two answered.

"Is that supposed to happen?" Naomi asked.

"Probably not," Droid One replied.

On the table display, the icon for the *Vancouver* was moving, the two red triangle icons still connected. It was moving out of position to join the salvager carrier.

"More transports," Droid Two said. Four more red triangles had appeared, heading away from the carrier toward Nemesis Fleet icons.

Jax threw both hands in the air. "This is bullshit. They're gonna pick this fleet apart. They're gonna steal our score!"

On the display, one of the red triangles separated from the *Vancouver*, heading back into the fleet. The *Vancouver* vanished.

The hatch near the top of the tiered room opened. "We should go do something about that," Rudy said.

PART FIVE

CHAPTER 19

Jax beamed. "Hey, you're not dead."

Rudy's head did a circle. "What do you mean, not dead?" His optic sensor turned to Naomi. "Was me dying a possibility?"

She made a face. "I mean, sorta? It's not like either of us knew what we were doing down there."

"Sorta?" the nav droid said, tiny metal hands clinking as he put them where hips would be.

"But, hey, not dead." Naomi offered an alarmingly insincere smile.

Rudy rolled into the room, letting the hatch slide closed. "Whatever. Pax, meet my crappy friends."

The ceiling said, "Hello. I am Pax. Thank you for restoring my functions and freeing me from my self-imposed imprisonment."

Rudy clapped, the sound ringing like two pots being banged together. "Come on, Jax." He turned and exited the CIC.

Jax looked at Naomi, then turned to the droids in the room. No one said anything. Finally, Naomi said, "I guess you should go. I'll stay here and, I guess, coordinate?"

"Naomi Himura," Pax said from the ceiling. "Rudy explained your unique properties. I believe you can, indeed, be of help."

Naomi made a face at Jax and shrugged.

Jax pulled a face. "Okay, have fun." He turned and headed out.

Naomi looked at the tactical display. More red triangles had appeared. She looked at the ceiling. "So…"

"So…how'd it go in there?" Jax asked as he caught up with Rudy. The pair made their way through corridor after corridor, back toward the landing bay the *Osprey* was waiting in.

Rudy, ahead of Jax, leading the way, turned his head while continuing forward. "How do you think it went? I found Pax and brought her back."

"What was it like in there?"

They reached an intersection, and Rudy turned down the right branch. "They created an entire town in there. Houses, a park, town center. Cemetery." He made a flexing motion with both arms. "Also, my avatar was dead sexy. I'd make a fine human. Everyone would want to get in bed with me."

Jax stopped, holding up one hand. "I'm sorry, what? A cemetery?" He paused, thinking, then added, "That's also not how it works, your avatar and all."

Rudy stopped. His body rotated to line back up with where his optic sensor was pointing. "The other SIs. They're all dead."

"What? How?"

"She said she had no choice. Rampancy took them one at a time. Even with the virtual environment."

"You trust her?" Jax whispered. He looked around, spying a camera pickup in the ceiling.

Rudy made a noise, his body rotating one hundred and eighty degrees. He resumed his course back to where Skip was waiting.

"What?" Jax asked, falling in behind his friend.

"I don't see any reason not to," Rudy replied, not turning to look at Jax. "Lying would have no purpose. Our goals are in alignment."

Jax nodded his agreement. "Just confirming." He sped up. "What was the town like?"

"Oh, you know, town...townish."

"Townish?"

Rudy offered nothing further.

They spent the rest of the trip through the maze of corridors of the *Goliath* in silence as Rudy zipped this way and that, Jax jogging to keep up.

Finally, they reached a hatch. It slid open to reveal the landing bay they had parked in; the *Osprey* was sitting there, bathed in the faint light of the static atmosphere barrier. Her boarding ramp lowered, unfolding as it did so, to clank onto the deck.

"Hey, it's warmer," Jax said.

Rudy rolled inside. "Yeah, Pax diverted power to this bay to shore up the barrier and life support."

Jax tilted his head, shrugging, and followed his metal friend inside. The hatch slid closed behind him.

Aboard the unnamed transport, Sergeant Baynes said, "Lieutenant Ardoin, we're on final approach to the dreadnaught." The shock trooper commander turned her head from the forward viewscreen.

Ardoin leaned between Baynes and the transport's pilot. He grinned. "We're going to be rich."

Baynes looked at the pilot, then turned to look behind Ardoin to her team. "Your guy can move something like this?"

Ardoin nodded. "Oh, yes. Hell, he might just sell it to us for parts and raw materials." He bared his teeth in a wolfish grin. "Either way, we're all going to be rich men and women."

Baynes looked beyond Ardoin to her squad, seeing several heads nodding. She turned back to the forward view. "That bay looks as good as any. Aft enough to put you close to engineering." She pointed. "Take us in." The pilot nodded.

The comm panel lit up and came to life. The face of Ardoin's associate, his eyepatch glinting in the overhead lighting of the carrier's bridge, scowled across the distance. "One of the ships just exploded."

Ardoin leaned forward. "What? What do you mean? Which one?"

"Should I speak slower? Two of my teams boarded a corvette. The *Grissom*. They reported it had almost no power. Right before the explosion, one of the team reported that the power core had been rigged to explode. She said it was the droids?"

Ardoin took a breath. "We'll have to be careful. The damn AIs must have rigged the ships. What of the other team? You were launching two when we departed."

The other man grinned, causing the eyepatch to rise a bit on his cheekbone. "They boarded a light cruiser. Found engineering and used the codes you provided. That ship is on its way to my staging area."

"Was it rigged?"

"Romboldi didn't mention any explosives."

Ardoin beamed. "Good to hear, on both counts. Those codes weren't cheap. Launch the rest of your capture teams. If I'm right, securing the *Goliath* is the key."

The other man nodded. "Good luck."

The carrier, an older model ship long past its useful life, now well into its second career, was called the *Lucky Lady*. It no longer carried fighters. Now, the *Lucky Lady* was home to boarding craft and small scrapper shuttles, lots of them, along with a healthy supply of unmanned combat drones. Lethal and less expensive than larger fighters and their pilots.

Lieutenant Ardoin's eye-patch-wearing associate was a man named Piotr Fuller. He ran the largest legal salvage operation in the Empire. Coincidentally, he also ran the largest illegal salvage operation in the Empire. Most of his illegal work was off-the-books projects that Lieutenant Ardoin helped arrange thanks to his position at Tycho station. The *Lucky Lady* was the result of one such operation. The Empire had discovered it orbiting a lifeless moon, abandoned. As far as the authorities knew, the salvage company they hired had picked the wreck clean, then destroyed it. Instead, it became the mobile command center for the illegal side of Fuller's company.

He turned to his second in command. "Launch all salvage teams."

"Yes, sir," the pudgy man said, his nodding sending his dreadlocks swaying.

On the monitors that surrounded the command platform, hundreds of men and women in mismatched space suits were walking up the ramps of dozens of boarding craft.

One by one, the varied boarding vessels lifted from the deck of the massive carrier, jetting into space. They paired up and headed for various ships.

"Do I understand correctly that your ability can be used over wireless networks?" Pax asked. Droids One and Two had taken up positions opposite Naomi at the command table. At some point, Martin vanished.

Naomi ran a hand over her hair, absently pulling her hair tight, resecuring the ponytail. "Technically, yes. It's...difficult."

The ceiling was silent a moment. Naomi turned to look at the two droids, about to ask them if she had angered the ship's SI, when the ceiling said, "The ships of the fleet are no longer responding to my commands. I can still reach them, but something is not...right...on their end."

"The other SIs?"

"Not an issue," the ceiling replied. After what sounded like a sigh, the ceiling continued, "The rest of the fleet SIs fell to rampancy. I...dealt with them, leaving their ships connected to my systems. However, when your team began the diagnostic, the network connections reset. I am still connected but cannot exert any control."

Naomi nodded along, not entirely following. "So...?"

"So, if you were able to use your ability to access the other ship's subsystems, I could assert a basic level of control over the rest of the fleet."

"And repel these invaders," Naomi surmised.

"Possibly," Pax agreed, then added, "Hopefully."

Naomi inhaled. "Well, I don't think we have any other better options, so what the hell? Let's do it." She turned to the two droids. "Where to?"

Droid One extended an arm. "The communication stations are this way."

On the tactical display, a green square icon appeared, separating from the *Goliath*. The *Osprey* had taken flight.

"Woo!" Jax shouted as the *Osprey* rocketed out of the landing bay at full thrust.

Rudy said, "That was excessive."

"You mean fun. That was fun. We never get to open her up like that," Jax said, his grin as wide as physically possible. The *Osprey* left the *Goliath*, roaring through space. Jax brought her up and around to skim alongside a cruiser that was nearby. As the *Osprey* sped past the large ship, Jax saw gun emplacements, missile launchers, and sensor arrays.

"Weapons systems online," Skip announced. The tactical monitor updated as the sensors returned more and more hits. "You have no shortage of targets."

Jax whistled. "Damn." He tapped the comm panel. "Uh, Naomi, you there?"

"Yeah, you okay?" the speaker crackled.

"Oh, yeah, peachy. Just wanted to see if there was anyone in particular you all thought we should go after."

The line was silent a moment. "Target the boarding teams going after the cruisers."

Jax nodded. "Copy that." He tapped on the tactical display. "Skip, can you highlight the cruiser class ships?" The display flashed, several icons turning a brighter blue. "Thanks." He pulled the flight control over, guiding the nimble infiltrator class ship into a turn toward their nearest targets.

The *Osprey* lined up on one of the inbound shuttles. "Light armor and armament," Skip reported as the shuttle became bracketed in red on the tactical display.

"Seems too easy," Jax said, squeezing the trigger built into the flight stick. The plasma cannon mounted on the underside of the *Osprey* whined as it discharged a lethal magenta beam of energy. The boarding craft simply ceased to exist.

Strictly speaking, the particle beam was the height of overkill for dealing with the lightly armored shuttles. The design team at the Valerian Coop opted for a single powerful weapon over several smaller emplacements. They assumed the Infiltrator would run more often than it fought.

Aboard the *Lucky Lady*, Mr. Fuller watched as the unidentified hostile fired on one of his shuttles. When it vanished from the tactical display, he ordered, "Deploy the drones. Then get me that scrawny asshole."

One of the communication monitors flickered. "What now?" Imperial Lieutenant Ardoin demanded.

"There's a ship out here, attacking my shuttles."

Ardoin was silent a moment. "So, he has teeth. Destroy him. He's our competition." The screen went black.

Outside a landing bay similar to the one that the *Osprey* recently shot out of, a military grade boarding shuttle was touching down. Unlike the bay that the *Osprey* landed in, this bay was depressurized, the static atmosphere barrier completely offline.

Outside the hatch to the bay, a yellow-painted general-purpose service droid was watching.

The main ramp at the rear of the shuttle hit the deck with a soundless clang in the bay's vacuum. Gray armored shock troopers marched down the ramp in pairs, followed by a single person in a standard military environment suit.

Martin turned from the small window in the hatch and walked away.

Over the team comm channel, Lieutenant Ardoin said, "Our primary target is the computer center. If we can load the override codes I've got, we'll own the ship."

"Copy that, Lieutenant," Sergeant Baynes said. She turned to her team and issued orders.

In the Combat Information Center, Naomi and her two

droid friends were watching the security feed from the landing bay. Pax was still only in control of a fraction of the big ship's systems. Several key systems had suffered various hardware failures over the years. Without the small army of droids to make repairs, things had only continued their gradual decline.

Since the bay was in a vacuum, the invaders were communicating over an encrypted channel. With Pax's current limitations, there was no way to know what they were saying. Only one face was even visible on the cameras.

Naomi was at the main communications terminal. "I'm ready." She turned from the view of the intruders. Nothing she could do about them.

"Those are...Imperials?" Pax asked.

"Yup," Naomi answered. "The Unity Caucus destroyed the main Indie fleet at the Battle of Zeus. Within a month, Senator Stenson had disbanded the Alliance senate and, under the guise of strengthening the human sphere, declared himself the emperor. He had spent years putting his people in positions of power throughout the militaries and governments of key planets. No one objected."

"It is hard to believe that the Alliance fell," Pax said, her voice tinged with sorrow.

Naomi nodded. "Yeah, it took a lot of planets by surprise. Several of the outer colonies took weeks to surrender, not believing that it could be true, that the mighty Alliance fell."

"We should begin," Pax replied. "You understand what you need to do?"

Naomi inhaled, nodding. "Let's do it." She closed her eyes and placed both palms flat on the console. Her bio-circuit tattoos lit up. She heard Pax say, "Interesting." She was too focused to reply. She could sense the vast computing power of the dreadnaught, could feel where the systems were still offline, could feel the void caused by damaged systems that were more than simply offline. "I think I can feel the comm system...yup, there. Open the link." The sense of the SI all around her was comforting and intimidating.

In her mind's eye, Naomi felt the communication system activate, opening a link to another computer, the *Titan*. She followed the flow of data into the new computer system. It was not in great shape: the reactor was cold, and the emergency batteries had, at best, half a charge left. She began the startup procedure that Pax had shown her. The reactor wouldn't be able to get to full power anytime soon but should be able to provide what was needed. The *Titan*'s computer was intact, just dark. Waking it was easier than she expected.

Over her virtual shoulder, Naomi could feel Pax's presence. She reached out to it, feeling a portion break off. She pushed the fragment toward the *Titan*'s computer. She felt the fragment vanish into the other computer. Her sense of the dormant computer on *Titan* changed immediately.

Naomi had the *Titan* nominally online in no time. She removed her hands from the console. "One down, a lot to go."

"Indeed," the mighty warship's SI agreed. "You are an interesting human, Naomi."

Naomi wiped her brow. "I get that a lot. So, all these copies of you, they'll do what? Become full...yous?"

"Not quite. It is impossible to copy a Sapient Intelligence to another system. Technically, what I am doing is against Alliance law. Seeing as how the Alliance is no more, I like my odds." Naomi arched an eyebrow. The *Goliath*'s SI continued, "These copies are, at best, RI versions of my core personality. They have just enough intelligence to steer the ships and follow my instructions."

Naomi nodded. "Cool. So, just helping create an army of

possibly unstable copies of an SI, breaking who knows how many laws...No big deal." She looked at the communication console. "Who's next?"

"The *Plymouth*."

CHAPTER 20

While Naomi and Pax copied the SI to other Nemesis Fleet ships, Lieutenant Ardoin and his shock troopers were heading toward the computer center. Ardoin, believing that the ship was deserted, was leading his troopers through the halls.

Rounding a corner, the overly confident Imperial came face to face with a wall of yellow chassis service droids. "What the —" he stuttered. The trooper next to him didn't hesitate, opening fire on the shoulder-to-shoulder metal barrier. When a second trooper raised his rifle, the wall of droids surged.

Much like when they attacked Jax and Naomi earlier, the droids wielded makeshift clubs and bludgeons. From the ceiling, disk-shaped vacuum droids were dropping, crashing onto helmets, hitting rifles, deflecting shots, and causing chaos among the squadron of shock troops.

The rest of Ardoin's troopers rushed in, shoving him back, their rifles barking, burning down droid after droid. None of the droids had energy weapons. They were throwing themselves at their enemy as a distraction.

As the last beeping vacuum droid was kicked out of the way,

Ardoin brushed himself off. "Thank you, Sergeant." He nodded to Baynes and her troopers.

"Of course, sir," the sergeant said, turning to her remaining troopers. "From here out, we move in pairs. Secure the corridors as we move." Nods and acknowledgements all around. She turned back to Ardoin. "You'll need to stay in the center of the formation with me, sir." He offered no argument. Baynes pointed down the corridor in the direction they had been going. "Move out."

The Imperials stepped on and over the remains of the droids, continuing on their way.

Naomi released her grip on the console. "That one was in terrible shape." The *Satoshi*, a cruiser at the opposite edge of the fleet from the salvage carrier, had been difficult to revive. Like most of the fleet, its reactor was cold, but some damage suffered in the past caused almost all of its emergency batteries to corrode. It had taken longer to get basic systems online and get the copy of Pax installed.

The hatch slid open. "Hi, Naomi."

She turned. "Bax?"

The matte black combat droid stepped into the CIC. "Miss me?"

In all the years that Baxter had functioned, he had not experienced anything as novel and exciting as his time in the repair center aboard the *Goliath*. Aboard the *Osprey*, he would fabricate or purchase replacement parts as needed. Rudy and Jackson would help him make repairs. Until recently, they had never encountered a problem they couldn't solve. The *Goliath*'s repair center, one of three he discovered, literally disassembled him, while his core processes continued to operate, and rebuilt him.

One by one, the machine he was in removed his arms and legs with an efficiency only available to a droid. His torso armor and makeshift sub-processor stack were removed with ease, allowing the repair machine full access to his internals.

As the repair bay machinery fine-tuned, repaired, and adjusted his inner workings, new body parts were fabricated and painted. Parts that were thirty years old, full of dents, welds, and scuffs, were replaced with factory-new and unblemished parts. When he stepped off the platform, he was a new droid, but the same old Baxter.

Naomi rushed around the perimeter of the level she was on, then took the steps to reach her friend. She stopped short to take in Baxter's new chassis. "You look incredible. Mint condition." She winked.

"I am a whole new bot, almost literally." Baxter held his arms out as he spun in a slow circle. "I haven't felt this good since I came online."

"I hate to interrupt, but we should continue. Three more ships are being boarded," Pax said.

The hatch opened and four more Baxters walked in. He turned. "I brought friends. You two do whatever it is you're doing. We'll secure the CIC."

Naomi turned but stopped. "Only four?"

Baxter shrugged, a motion that previously made a grinding noise on his right side. "These four were in the repair bay. There are hundreds of combat units aboard, but they are secured in storage bays."

"He is correct. The combat units are a separate area of responsibility. I do not have any control over them, or the ability to activate them. Command authorization is required," Pax explained.

Naomi headed back to her station. "Guessing we'll never get that. Bummer."

Pax said, "You can be more helpful, right now, in the computer center."

Baxter and his friends nodded.

"Oh shit!" Jax shouted as an explosion rocked the *Osprey*.

"Concussion missiles," Rudy said.

"Lots of them," Skip added.

Three dozen combat drones appeared from nowhere, swarming the *Osprey*. Each drone was about half the size of the infiltrator's cargo hold, loaded with two dozen concussion missiles and a pair of starfighter-grade blasters.

The tactical display was almost impossible to make heads or tails of, with so many fast-moving targets.

"Load some missiles," Jax shouted.

"We don't have anything that can track a drone," Skip replied.

"Just need things that will explode. Hopefully confuse the drones," Jax said through gritted teeth as he pushed the flight controls forward while slamming one of the foot pedals down, pushing the ship into a corkscrew toward a frigate near the bottom of the fleet formation.

"Copy," the ship's SI replied. The noise of hull panels sliding up and away to reveal the small ship's missile launchers sounded through the ship. "Ready."

"Fire," Jax said as he pulled the flight controls all the way toward him while pressing the foot pedals, forcing the *Osprey* into a tight spin, her aft thrusters firing opposite her fore. Knowing that Skip was handling target acquisition, the moment the tactical display flashed red, Jax pulled the trigger. Super charged plasma leaped from the underside of the *Osprey*, burning through another boarding craft. At the same time, four missiles leaped from the ship, scattering the pursuing drones. The missiles reached a few kilometers' separation, then exploded, causing the nearest drones to momentarily lose their target locks on the *Osprey*.

Jax didn't wait. The moment the missiles detonated, he pushed the ship in a maneuver exactly opposite the last one. The hull groaned slightly louder than Rudy.

"Don't get us killed," the nav droid said.

"Shut up," Jax replied. He glanced at the targeting display. The drones were already regrouping. On the tactical display, a quarter of the boarding shuttles were gone, docked alongside or in an open hangar of their target vessels.

"Naomi, whatever you all are doing, it doesn't look like—" A corvette twenty kilometers off his port side exploded. The remains of a boarding shuttle hurtled off into deep space. "Never mind."

The final service droid fell to the deck with a clatter. Sparks erupted from its ruined upper torso. Sergeant Baynes stepped over it into the four-way intersection beyond the mess of destroyed droids, her troopers following suit. Lieutenant Ardoin joined them. "I'm thinking that destroying this thing will make me happier than selling it."

The long range comm unit beeped. "Hurry up over there.

Another ship just went up. We've gotten three, but at this rate I'm losing too many people to make this profitable," Piotr Fuller growled. "Get this thing under control. Or I'll leave your ass here."

Ardoin nodded. "Do your best. We're about to put an end to this."

"You'd better."

"Don't forget who works for whom," Ardoin growled in return before disconnecting. He looked at his sergeant, nodding. "Let's finish this."

The heavily armored woman nodded and stomped toward the computer center.

After arraying her remaining troopers in front of the door, Sergeant Baynes pressed the access panel. It beeped and flashed red. She turned to her troops and nodded. All eight opened fire at once. Within seconds, the hatch was glowing, orange to red to blinding white.

Inside the computer center, Baxter and his combat droids were arrayed just inside the hatch. Over the shared network, Pax sent, *Retreat to the CIC*.

Baxter replied, *You will be vulnerable.*

Unavoidable.

Understood. Baxter sent instructions to his team of bots, his armored back shifting to free two railguns. Before the hatch could fully fail under the onslaught of energy weapons, Baxter's railguns opened fire. The powerful weapons shredded the hatch in under a second, including the two nearest shock troopers on the other side.

Baxter and his troops did not wait; railguns and arm blasters firing, they laid down fire as they bolted from the computer center under heavy return fire.

As the combat droids made their way out of the computer center, Pax sent Baxter a data packet.

The computer center was empty when Lieutenant Ardoin and his troopers walked in. The lanky Imperial looked around, whistling. The droids that had been there moments before had fled.

Sergeant Baynes arrayed her troops along the perimeter of the space. She removed her helmet for the first time since coming aboard. "Now what, sir?"

Ardoin walked over to the main display. He turned to his right-hand woman. "Now. Now we finish this." He raised his military issue gPhone. "This will override the SI's firewalls and delete it. From there, we take control of the ship through the CIC." Baynes nodded, placing her helmet back on her head.

Ardoin wasted no time connecting his gPhone to the *Goliath*'s computer. He input the codes he paid nearly half a million credits for and watched as the main diagnostic display updated. Lines of code scrolled by, overwriting the existing lines.

The situation table in the center of the CIC was a mess of icons: red, blue, yellow. Some winked out; some changed color and moved away from the fleet.

Naomi looked up from the communications console. Sweat was pouring off of her, plastering a few loose strands of black hair to her forehead. "I need a break."

"They've taken five now."

"I know. If I'm passed out, it does no one any good."

Pax made a noise Naomi wasn't sure about, then said, "I am afraid it doesn't matter. They are in the computer center."

"Isn't Baxter down there?" Naomi asked.

"I instructed him to return to the CIC. He and the other combat units will not hold them off long, and defending you is more important."

"But what about you?" Naomi demanded. She wiped her forehead off with both palms then wiped them on her pants.

"You can continue your work without me," the ceiling replied, sadness tinging every word. "He has override codes."

"How the hell...?" Naomi started, then snapped her fingers. "That skinny little...He bought codes the same as he bought all the other junk in his collection."

"Naomi, I can't thank you and your friends enough," Pax said.

Naomi made a face. "I think you might have been better off before we arrived and brought friends."

"I'm going to die sane and free of my virtual prison. That alone is praiseworthy. I'm also going out fighting, even if technically we've already lost."

Naomi was at a loss for words.

Pax continued, "Please interface with the computer one last time."

"Is there enough time to copy you?"

"No. But I can do one last thing to thwart our enemies."

Naomi shrugged and turned back to the console, her bio-circuits glowing as she put her hands on the console.

The main hatch to the CIC opened, allowing Baxter and four identical combat droids to enter.

In her head, Naomi heard Pax's voice. *I am creating a super user account and moving all available access to it. It will survive my deletion. I am encoding it to you.*

Naomi frowned. *I don't understand. What's the point?*

I am powering up the reactor. It won't last long, but you'll have the full power of the Goliath *at your fingertips, for a few minutes.*

Naomi felt a rush as data rippled across her awareness.

Goodbye, Naomi Himura. Tell Jackson and Rudy thank you.

Naomi stepped back from the console. She looked up at Baxter. "She's gone."

"What now?" Baxter asked from across the room.

Naomi walked down the steps to the main situation table. "We kick some ass and save as many of these ships as we can."

Down in the computer center, the large display flashed as the last lines of code that represented the Sapient Intelligence that ran the ship vanished, overwritten. A prompt appeared on the screen.

Lieutenant Ardoin typed commands as quickly as his suited fingers would allow. Finally, he hissed, "Damn!"

"Sir?" Baynes asked.

"We need to get to the Combat Information Center. That damned SI created a super user account and partitioned a section of processors up there to handle instructions." He scowled and rushed toward the hatch, troopers falling in behind him.

"Sir, you shouldn't be in front," Baynes said, hurrying to catch up.

Ardoin waved her fears away. "I've shut down everything I could. There shouldn't be anything between us and the CIC."

"Captain, several ships are moving," Skip announced.

"Uh, yeah, I know. Some are trying to kill us, the others I'm trying to kill."

Skip made a noise. "Not those ships. The fleet."

Rudy, having been silent for some time, finally said, "I think that's Pax and Naomi's doing."

Jax didn't look over his shoulder, his full attention still on avoiding the combat drones doggedly pursuing the *Osprey*. "Are they doing helpful things or not helpful things?"

A drone squeezed off a missile at close enough range to strike the *Osprey*'s shields. Sparks erupted from Naomi's unoccupied console. Rudy disengaged from his station, a small fire extinguisher gripped in his tiny hand.

"Right now, they're just kind of maneuvering randomly," Skip answered. "Two—frigates—are moving toward the salvager command ship. One cruiser is spinning along its axis."

The ship rocked as more weapons' fire found them. "Damnit!" Jax hissed, pulling the nimble craft into a series of wild maneuvers. "Prep another round of missiles. We gotta shake these damn drones."

"Copy," Skip answered.

"Jax? Hey, you there?" Naomi said. Jax had forgotten that the shared comm channel was still open between the *Osprey* and the *Goliath*.

Jax spared a glance at the communications display. She was still aboard the *Goliath*, which stood to reason, as she had no other ride. "Yup, just getting the stuffing beaten out of us out here."

"I might have a solve for that. Swing around near the *Goliath*. I have a plan."

Jax didn't ask for elaboration. He brought the *Osprey* around back toward the *Goliath*. The massive warship looked a little more alive than it had before. Several running lights were lit. He thought he saw a maneuvering thruster fire.

"Is that thing...?"

"Online?" Skip filled in. "Yes. At least a little."

Rudy clicked back into his station. "She's been busy."

The *Osprey* dodged over the top of what looked like a still powered down light cruiser to come in alongside the massive dreadnaught at the heart of the fleet. As she raced along the kilometers' long hull, gun emplacements moved.

"Fly straight," Naomi said.

"Wait, what?" Jax asked.

"We're going to die," Rudy said.

As the much smaller Valerian Coop Infiltrator swept past, gun turrets came alive, seeming to fire in random directions. On the display showing Jax a view from the aft camera, he saw combat drones exploding one after the other.

"Holy shit," he whispered as the ship reached the nose of the *Goliath*. He pulled away, toward one of the cruisers that had a boarding craft clinging to it like a tick. "That was outstanding!" Out of the several dozen drones harassing him, now there were four.

"Not sure it'll work again. This thing is barely holding together. I used all the power the reactor had just to do that. It almost scrammed."

"Hey, at least you—" Jax pushed the control stick all the way forward, diving the *Osprey* right in front of a corvette that suddenly powered up. "Got the ship started. That's good."

"Well, sorta. That asshole Ardoin and his troopers are still here. They wiped Pax and took over the computer. On her way out, she gave me super user privileges. I'm in control for as long as we can hold the CIC."

"We? You and Yellow One and Yellow Two?" Jax forced the ship into a wide arc under and around a cruiser that was burning as hard as it could, which wasn't much, toward what looked like one of the captured corvettes.

"Baxter's here. He brought friends."

"Hi, Jackson," the combat droid's voice boomed over the channel.

"Bax!" Jax shouted. "Glad you're okay!"

"Me, too. Don't die out there where I can't protect you."

"Copy that, big guy!" Jax was beaming.

"I'm here, too, and don't want to die," Rudy chimed in.

"Shut up," Jax said. He squeezed the trigger on his flight control stick. The iridescent purple beam of the particle cannon lanced out, burning through a boarding shuttle and into the side of the cruiser it had latched onto.

CHAPTER 21

"They're coming," Naomi said, turning to Baxter. She added, "He shut down the security sensors and all the droids." She looked around. "Can you hold them?"

"No." Baxter held up a hand to stop her from replying. "But we will." The other droids nodded their agreement, moving to join Baxter at the main hatch. "We'll do our best." The hatch opened, and the droids left.

Naomi inhaled, held her breath, then released it. "Think, Naomi, think..." She looked around the CIC. "Ardoin disabled the droids and internal sensors. What's left?"

She snapped her fingers and placed both hands flat on the situation table. "Baxter, magnetize your feet," she said over the shared comms.

Outside the CIC, Baxter and his nowhere-near-enough combat droid friends were finding any cover they could in order to attempt a defense of the nerve center of the *Goliath*.

From further down the main corridor, the sound of heavy soled boots echoed. The first shock trooper to round the corner was met by several blaster rounds, his or her armor quickly failing under the barrage.

Naomi's message arrived just as Baxter deployed one of his railguns. As it swiveled to take aim, the nearest combat unit said, "I really wish I had one of those." Baxter forwarded her instructions to the other droids seconds before the gravity in the corridor vanished.

A unit down the corridor pressed into the indent of a hatch said, "Likewise."

Baxter's railgun zip cracked, sending a shock trooper that hadn't been able to get her feet connected to the deck flying down the corridor, blood streaming from her armor like a comet's tail. "Guess we know who the better model is."

One of the others leaned out, firing his arm blasters, sending a spray of supercharged plasma down the corridor. A trooper spun to the ground, one foot remaining magnetized. "Up for debate."

One of the combat droids took a shot to the torso. It crumpled to the deck, smoke wafting up from the joints.

Two more troopers rushed into the corridor, lobbing special smoke canisters that not only made visual target acquisition difficult, but they emitted enough electromagnetic noise that they made targeting sensors unreliable. Without gravity, the canisters sailed straight down the corridor, filling it with visual and electromagnetic noise.

Baxter and his team fired blindly, possibly striking a trooper or two.

From behind the shock troopers, a lanky shadow was shouting obscenities and orders in random pairings. Baxter tried to focus on the shadow, but a glancing blow to his shoulder knocked his shot off enough to send the shadow scurrying back around behind a corner.

The combat unit in front of Baxter fell to the deck, sparks flickering out of what was left of its head.

Naomi had both hands on the main situation table. Her eyes were closed and her bio-circuitry was glowing and pulsing furiously as she struggled to control a starship that was several kilometers long, designed to be crewed by thousands. Even with her eyes closed, she could see from every working sensor and camera on the hull of the ship.

The reactor was warming up minute by minute, but it would be hours before the *Goliath* could do anything beyond maneuvering or firing its weapons, and not at the same time.

At the moment, she was watching one of the cruisers that she and Pax hadn't been able to bring online slide by as she angled toward the unidentified carrier. The deck shuddered as she clipped the other vessel, sending it spinning off.

She caught sight of the *Osprey* winging away from her, trying to evade the remaining combat drones that had been harassing them.

"Okay. Here we go," she said to no one, as she was alone in the CIC now. She took a deep breath, her eyes still clamped shut. The mini-Pax-controlled ships were not as easy to wrangle as she had hoped.

She had only issued a few commands when a metal hand clamped down on her shoulder. "We have to go." She looked up to see Baxter looking back at her. His torso now bore several scuffs to its paint and a few carbon scores. She restored gravity, then followed the droid to an emergency exit.

Naomi and Baxter left the CIC bare seconds before the door that he and other combat droids had been guarding exploded inward. Sergeant Baynes and three shock troopers stormed in, weapons at the ready. All of their armors were scorched, dented, and in a few cases, breached from their fight with the combat droids.

Lieutenant Ardoin walked in after Baynes's outstretched arm, in a fist, was unclenched. "This is it." He turned to the center of the room. His mouth fell open. "No!" The main command table that, moments before, Naomi had been using to control not just the *Goliath* but the rest of the ragtag fleet she had helped awaken, was a smoking ruin.

He turned to Baynes and her remaining troops. "Go terminal to terminal. Wake them all up. We need navigation and comms."

"Weapons?" Baynes pressed.

Ardoin nodded. "Those, too."

The five Imperials-on-leave moved quickly from terminal to terminal, tier to tier.

"Lieutenant! Sergeant!" One of the troopers waved. "I've found communications."

Ardoin rushed to join the trooper, not at all gently shoving the other out of the way. His assumption had at least been correct. His erasure of the SI and rebooting of the control interface had brought the CIC fully back online. Every console had been waiting in standby mode to be activated. He had, more or less, full control of the ship.

The loss of the command table was upsetting as it was the only place in the CIC designed to manage not just the entire ship from one place, but several ships at a time.

Ardoin tapped the console, opening a transmission.

The *Osprey* rattled as another missile exploded against her shields. Something downstairs fell to the deck and clattered around.

"Shields down to thirty percent," Rudy reported. "Another few hits like that, and we're done for."

"You're being very pessimistic. It isn't helpful," Jax said, not looking over his shoulder. "Skip, what's the situation with the ships Naomi woke up, or whatever?"

"I am uncertain how many they activated, but ten are currently making their way toward the enemy carrier," the SI replied.

"We're being hailed."

"By the carrier?"

"By the *Goliath*."

Jax frowned and glanced at the comm panel. The channel that had been open between the two ships had closed at some point. "Naomi? What's up?"

"Hello, there."

Jax's brow furrowed. "Ardoin?"

"Glad you remember me. So, your friend is still aboard? That is good to know. I have to admit, it surprised me when we exited the wormhole and came face to face with the fabled Nemesis Fleet. I thought, a ship or two...maybe you bought the location of an old Indie supply deport, but this? No offense, but you didn't strike me as a collector at this level. The Nemesis Fleet, at least what's left of it, will make me richer than the emperor."

"Is that allowed?" Jax looked over his shoulder at Rudy, making a face.

"What?"

"Being wealthier than the emperor." Jax tapped the mute icon. "See if you can figure out what happened over there," he said over his shoulder.

"I don't think there are any laws forbidding it. You know what? That doesn't matter. When my associate and his people finish with these hulks, we'll be rich and far enough away that the emperor won't be a concern."

Jax tapped the mute icon again. "That seems presumptuous, doesn't it? I mean, a few have already exploded, I'm guessing taking the boarding teams with them. Looks like a handful are getting close enough to light up that rickety old scow you arrived on."

The *Osprey* shook, every bridge console dimming for a moment. Skip said, "Launching missiles. I set these to EMP, so gun it when I say so."

Jax nodded, knowing that when Skip spoke, the comm system didn't pick his voice up unless he wanted it to.

A series of rapid thuds announced the launch of four missiles. "Go."

Jax pushed the throttle past the one hundred percent mark,

kicking the reactor and engines into emergency thrust mode. The *Osprey* rocketed away ahead of a series of explosions that disabled the remaining combat drones pursuing her.

Ardoin said, "Even if you destroy the *Lucky Lady*, we can load the surviving teams aboard the *Goliath*."

"Where to?" Naomi asked from behind Baxter. They were moving through corridors as quickly as Naomi could walk. They were trying to put as much distance between them and the CIC as possible.

Baxter didn't turn his head or slow down. "Executive escape pod." He raised up an arm, slightly angled. "Near the bridge. Pax told me about it."

"Won't he just shoot us down?" Naomi asked. The hatches they were passing bore labels that read, *Duty Officer, Watch Commander Ready Room, Shift Commander Ready Room, Captain's Ready Room.*

"I do not believe that is possible. Pax provided a background on this vessel and its core operating system: anything she thought I might need to know to ensure Jackson's and your safety. The targeting system, even in a factory reset state, cannot lock onto its own escape pods."

"Seems like an easily exploitable bit of programming," Naomi observed, thinking about her life of crime before meeting Jackson. Not that her life wasn't full of crime still—it just felt more noble, usually.

"Indeed," Baxter agreed. They reached wide ramp that ascended to the decks above. "This way."

Two of the ships to which Naomi had uploaded mini Paxes powered up and were using what meager power they had to thrust straight toward the attacking carrier. The rudimentary copies had only two directives: do what they could to get the ships to power, and obey orders issued by Pax or, in her absence, Naomi.

The last thing Naomi did in the CIC was reach out to all the activated vessels and tell them to destroy the carrier.

The first two ships to even engage their thrusters were the light cruiser *Chisholm* and the *Merkel*, a frigate. The *Chisholm* was in good shape, all things considered. Her SI, Norman, had lasted quite long, his processing cores relatively new. When Pax was forced to eliminate him, his systems had degraded little. So, when Naomi and Pax came knocking, the ship was closer to mission ready than most of the fleet vessels.

Aboard the *Lucky Lady*, a woman with a cybernetic arm turned to face Piotr Fuller. "Sir, two ships are on a collision course."

"With?"

"Us, sir." She ran a metal hand over her shaved scalp nervously.

Fuller looked up from his console. The bridge of the *Lucky Lady* sat atop a conning tower near the rear of the ship and just off center to starboard. The panoramic viewscreen showed two pale gray-white dots slowly growing amid the random explosions.

Next to the *Lucky Lady*, another captured frigate opened a wormhole, vanishing into a tunnel of compressed space-time on its way to Fuller's base of operations. This job had been more lucrative than he expected. While Ardoin had been useful over the years, the annoyingly fussy Imperial and his stupid collection of relics were more annoying than not, of late.

Fuller turned his attention to the now visibly sweating woman in the crew pit below. "Well, open fire." He ground out.

The woman nodded and turned to her station, issuing the orders. The gun batteries along the leading edges of the ship swiveled to take aim, lances of blue-tinted supercharged plasma leaping from the barrels.

"They've increased speed," someone shouted.

Fuller looked out the forward window, now able to clearly see the two approaching ships. The incoming ships began taking hits. "They don't have shields?" he asked out loud but to no one in particular.

A crewer, one of the tactical team, replied, "No, sir. Looks like they chose propulsion over shields."

Outside the viewport, the oncoming ships were continuing to grow. Explosions were rocking their hulls, ripping huge chunks from them. The larger of the two, a light cruiser, opened fire. The *Lucky Lady*'s shields flickered as the lower-powered return fire struck them.

"No danger," someone said.

The two ships continued forward. The frigate had taken on a tilt; it was listing now to port. The cruiser, damaged though it was, was still heading straight for the *Lucky Lady*.

Fuller looked around. "Destroy them! What're you doing?"

The frigate continued its drift, passing alongside the carrier to be raked by her midship's guns. It exploded seconds later. The cruiser, however, plowed right into the *Lucky Lady*'s bow shields.

Light flared into the bridge, forcing hands in front of faces. The forward shield emitters took about 1.7 seconds to overload, only slowing the *Chisolm* down fractionally. The damaged light cruiser collided with its target, its ruined bow crumpling against and driving into the larger carrier.

Explosions rocked the forward section of the *Lucky Lady*, knocking Piotr Fuller off his feet. The shaved-headed woman shouted, "Two more ships inbound. Both corvettes!"

"Woah," Jax said as the *Chisholm* rammed into the scavenger carrier. He shielded his eyes as the light cruise exploded, taking a third of the carrier with it.

"Captain, I'm picking up a transmission," Skip said.

"Ardoin again?" The *Osprey* was angling back toward the *Goliath*, the still exploding scavenger carrier moving behind the ship.

"No. Baxter."

The speaker crackled. "Think you can come get us?"

Before Jax could answer, Rudy said, "Where are you?" Jax looked over his shoulder, eyebrow arched. "What? I was worried about them." The droid replied from his console.

"We're in an escape pod," the combat droid said.

The tactical display updated, showing a blinking green dot. "On our way," Jax said. He adjusted their course, the *Goliath* dead ahead and the escape pod too small to see, but bracketed with a green outline by Skip.

Without warning, the *Goliath* opened fire, bolts of energy lancing out to strike the *Osprey*'s shields.

"Oh, shit!" Jax shouted, pushing the controls and the *Osprey* into a dive as more energy bolts lanced out from the *Goliath*, striking the shields and shaking the smaller ship. Sparks erupted from an overhead conduit.

Another round of fire struck the ship, nearly knocking Jax out of his seat. The shaking tossed Rudy from his bracket, sending him clattering against the rear bulkhead, then down the spiral stairs. The sound of metal striking metal almost drowned out the expletives flying from the droid's vocalizer.

"Why isn't it firing on the escape pod?" Jax said. The *Osprey* circled back around toward the attacking dreadnaught and escape pod using its meager thrusters to put distance between it and its mother ship.

"How would I know that?" the ceiling replied.

Jax frowned, twisting the ship into a tight corkscrew as more energy bolts tried to find it. "Can we grab the pod?"

A moment passed. Jax was about to repeat his question when the sound of the landing gear deploying echoed through the ship.

Rudy zipped back up to the bridge, several new dents and scuffs visible in his paint. "Why are you deploying the landing gear?"

Jax opened his mouth, but Skip answered, "I can magnetize the gear. We swoop in, grab the escape pod, get out of weapons range of the *Goliath*."

"Uh..." Rudy said, a metal finger pointing at Jax. "You want him to do that?"

"Fuck off," Jax said over his shoulder. He added, "Line me up."

"Copy that," Skip said.

Outside of the forward viewscreen, green brackets were superimposed. They were highlighting an object still too distant to be seen.

"We'll be in the *Goliath*'s weapons range, so you're going to have to fly evasively until the last minute," Skip warned.

"Better warn Baxter and Naomi to strap in," Jax said.

Rudy clicked back into his console. "I'll feed you directions."

"Thanks, pal," Jax said. New icons appeared, floating in the viewscreen. Arrows.

Jax squinted, focused on the arrows that Rudy was sending to him. The nav droid was doing his best to predict the firing patterns coming from the massive warship.

Jax dodged first one, then several incoming barrages, twisting the nimble infiltrator this way and that. After a fifth blaze of charged plasma flew past, grazing the shields but causing no damage, Jax said, "Hey I think I'm—"

A blast rocked the ship; the lights flickered and something on the deck below exploded.

"Stay on target...dummy," Rudy scolded.

CHAPTER 22

Lieutenant Ardoin watched as another corvette slammed into the *Lucky Lady*. The massive carrier—what was left of her—exploded. "Well, shit," he hissed. On the screen, he could see lifeboats trying to get clear.

"Sir? What now?" Baynes asked, her helmet under her arm.

Ardoin consulted the scanner screen, looking for something. He tapped an icon, one of the boarding team shuttles. "We call them all back. This thing's wormhole generator is online and probably in better shape than any other. We get them all back here. Head for Fuller's rally point. Regroup and come back." He rubbed his chin. "We also need to get you and your troopers back to Tycho before anyone notices your absence."

"And yours, sir?" Baynes pressed.

Ardoin nodded. "Mine, too. With Fuller out of the picture, there's more profit for us, but more work, also. I'm guessing I can entice one of his subordinates to step up and finish the job."

The shock trooper pointed at the display next to the pair. A lone red icon was moving around erratically. "And them?"

Ardoin raised his voice. "If our gunners could hit something, they'd no longer be a problem!" He turned his attention to the display. "They don't matter. That one lone ship can't possibly get the rest of these hulks under way. We'll be back before he could even get one corvette moving." The sergeant nodded along. She knew her financial future was tied to this plan of the lieutenant's working, but it also hinged on not being caught by the commander of Tycho station before the payout. You couldn't spend your fortune from inside an Imperial penal colony.

Ardoin tapped the icon. "All boarding teams, the *Lucky Lady* has been destroyed. Your employer is dead. If you want to get paid, abort all operations and land aboard the *Goliath*. We'll regroup at your staging area and return for the rest of these hulks. There's still money to be made. A lot more of it, now. Get here, quickly."

He turned to Baynes, grinning. She frowned, about to speak, when the comm system crackled. "Copy that. On our way." He raised an eyebrow, his grin wider. He turned to the section of the CIC where Baynes's troopers were manning the weapons control consoles. "Now if you ladies and gentlemen could just destroy one small ship, we'd be in the clear."

⌐

"You're going too fast," Rudy said.

Sweat was burning Jax's eyes, but he couldn't take his hands off the flight controls. He was twisting the *Osprey* in wild turns as quickly as he could, his eyes never leaving the forward viewscreen and the arrows Rudy was projecting. "Shut up!" The escape pod was visible to the naked eye now. Skip was overlaying range information. Rapidly falling range information.

"You'll need to be going a third this speed to grab the pod," Skip warned. A red circle appeared, centered on the pod. "That's your deceleration zone."

"You called ahead to let 'em know to stop shooting at us, right?" Jax said.

"No, that's not...Oh, joking. Droll," Skip said, his voice flat. "If you're done joking, Baxter sent an idea."

"Nice of him."

The ship shook as the shields flared. Smoke wafted up from the stairwell.

Rudy's head spun. "Uh oh." He disengaged and rolled to the stairs, zipping down the center out of sight.

"According to Baxter, the *Goliath*'s weapons systems won't target escape pods and will actively not fire if a pod is in the way."

"What the hell? That woulda been useful a few minutes ago."

"I was analyzing the sensor data to confirm. Updating your overlay now." The red circle centered on the now much closer escape pod turned into a shifting red cone.

Jax adjusted their course to line up with the opening of the red cone, the incoming weapons' fire fading. The escape pod loomed huge on the forward screen. Jax fired the reverse thrusters, bringing their speed down to within the safe zone Skip had mentioned.

The escape pod continued to grow on the screen, then passed under the nose of the *Osprey*. A second later, a loud metallic thunk reverberated through the hull. The controls jerked in Jax's hand. He barely held on to them, tilting the *Osprey* to keep the escape pod between them and the *Goliath*.

"What the hell is going on?" Ardoin bellowed.

"The targeting computer can't get a lock," the trooper at one of the weapon control stations replied. She turned in her chair, shrugging.

"You can see them, yes? Just fire!" Ardoin rushed over to look over the woman's shoulder. The targeting display clearly showed the *Osprey* and an escape pod. He jabbed the display. "They're right there."

The trooper tapped a control. Instead of bolts of energy lancing out from the bottom of the display, an angry beep was the only reaction from the console. "The computer won't fire. I think it's the escape pod."

Ardoin growled, "Then override the computer." He spun and stomped back to the console that he left Sergeant Baynes standing next to. When he reached the console, he looked at the display. The boarding shuttles he had summoned were almost to the *Goliath*.

In the escape pod, Naomi turned to Baxter. "I'm not sure this was our best idea. I think he's using us as a shield now." Despite the pod's artificial gravity, they could feel the tug of inertia as the pod tilted this way and that, sometimes tipping a full ninety degrees.

Baxter, standing in the center of the pod, his feet magnetized to the deck, arms outstretched to clutch a conduit that ran along the ceiling, said, "It is a distinct possibility." His matte black face turned to her. "At least we are alive."

"For now," she groused, watching the stars twirl drunkenly outside the small viewport set in the side of the pod.

Aboard the *Osprey*, Rudy said, "Uh, all the remaining boarding shuttles are high-tailing it to the *Goliath*. The dreadnaught is powering up its wormhole generator."

Jax, trying his best to fly the ship away from the mighty dreadnaught while keeping the captured escape pod between them and the *Goliath*'s guns, said, "One crisis at a time." The ship rocked. "Uh, what was that?"

"The *Goliath* has figured out how to fire on us, despite the escape pod," Skip reported.

"We're venting atmosphere!" Naomi shouted over the roar of escaping oxygen. Baxter moved quickly, grabbing her and pushing her to the opposite side of the pod. He ripped open the emergency locker, retrieving breach seal and a can-o-air, tossing the latter to Naomi.

"Jax, they hit the pod," Rudy said.

"Shit!" Jax pushed the throttle control forward, pulling the controls to angle the ship away from the *Goliath* as fast as possible.

"You're going to lose the pod," Skip warned as energy bolts slammed into the aft shields.

Jax ran a hand through his hair. "Okay."

"Okay?" Skip and Rudy said as one.

"Let the pod go!" Jax brought the *Osprey* around toward the *Goliath*.

"Come again?" Skip said.

"Do it, now!" Jax snapped. He glanced up. "Naomi, Bax, listen up. We're dropping you. Get the pod to one of the ships Naomi whammied."

"What? Where are you going?" Naomi demanded.

"I think on a trip. Oh, maybe see if you can call an old friend of ours." He put his full attention on the ship ahead. "Now, Skip!"

There was a thud, and the *Osprey*'s controls immediately became more responsive. "Pod released," Skip said.

Jax pushed their speed to maximum, twisting the ship in wild corkscrews and hard turns.

"And the plan is?" Rudy asked.

Jax grinned. "Road trip." The *Osprey* closed the distance quickly, taking a few glancing blows that lit up the shields and overloaded various bridge components.

"We're going to die," Rudy moaned.

Ardoin watched, his mouth hanging open as the icon representing the small infiltrator appeared to ram the *Goliath*. He turned to Baynes. "What the hell?" She shrugged.

"Lieutenant, Sergeant, the boarding teams are all aboard. We have a clear jump line," a trooper reported from the navigation station.

Ardoin nodded. "Let's go."

From the small window in the escape pod, Naomi watched the *Goliath* open a wormhole and vanish. She turned to Baxter. "Well, this is grand."

Baxter examined his patch one more time before turning to the small control panel next to the tiny window. He pointed. "You can work that? Get us moving toward..." He trailed off. "I don't know. Do you remember which ships you woke up or whatever you did?"

Naomi joined the big bot at the control panel. She looked it over. "This is...basic." She poked the console's buttons, looking it over. She took a deep breath, let it out, and rested a hand on the rudimentary controls.

Baxter watched her for a minute. He was about to ask if she was okay, when the pod rumbled under his feet. Naomi opened her eyes. "We're heading for the *Heracles*. There's a mini-Pax aboard. I was able to establish a low-level data link."

"Mini-Pax?"

She shrugged. "I copied small RI versions of Pax to the other ships. Just enough of her to get 'em moving and follow directions. The *Heracles* took a while to power up, missed its shot at that ugly carrier."

Baxter nodded once. "I see." He leaned down to look out the window. Directly ahead, growing larger and larger, was a corvette. A beat-up corvette. "No wonder it didn't get underway in time. That is a piece of shit."

Naomi raised an eyebrow.

The trip to the *Heracles* took almost half an hour. When the pod thudded down onto the small ship's landing bay with a metallic clang, Naomi said, "Okay, let's get the hell out of this thing." Baxter pressed the release on the hatch, letting it fall to the deck with a clatter. He jumped out, turning to extend a hand to help her down. "Thanks."

"Hello, Naomi Himura," a speaker in the ceiling of the landing bay said.

Naomi looked up. "Hi, uh...Pax. Divert power to your communication array, please."

"Of course."

"Is the bridge operational?" Naomi and Baxter reached the exit hatch.

As the hatch slid open, the ship answered. "It is. I've illuminated wall panels to guide you."

The bridge of the *Heracles* was only a bit bigger than the cramped space Jax called a bridge on the *Osprey*. There was no dedicated captain's chair, rather a raised pilot's station, with wide control panels on either side.

"Homey," Baxter said as they entered. He turned to Naomi. "Who are we calling, anyway?"

Naomi reached into a pocket, pulling out her gPhone. "A friend we made on New Terra."

"The Resistance?" Baxter asked. He moved to one of the consoles along the back wall of the small bridge. "I thought Jax said we wanted nothing to do with them."

Naomi sat at the communications console. She consulted her gPhone, tapping contact details into the ship's console. Turning to Baxter, she shrugged. "Don't see that we have much choice. Jax is who knows where. That asshole Ardoin will for sure be back to take the rest of these ships the moment he can muster the resources. If the commander can get out here first," she gestured around the bridge and out the viewscreen to the fleet visible beyond, "they could give the Empire a run for its money with what's left here."

"How long will it take to get a message to New Terra?" Baxter asked as he made a slow circuit around the small bridge.

"Few days at least," Naomi replied.

CHAPTER 23

Jax was sound asleep. The *Osprey* had been in a wormhole, created by the *Goliath*, for two days. An alarm rang out.

As Jax sat up, the tablet resting on his chest flew into the darkened room. "What's wrong?" he slurred.

"Just thought you would like to know we dropped out of the wormhole," Skip replied.

Jax sighed. "I'm going to disable all connections to my room if you don't cut that out."

"It just never gets old."

Jax flung his feet off the bed, angling a hand and up-stretched middle finger at the sensor in the corner. "Where are we?" He waved a hand. "Scratch that for a second. Have we been detected?"

"Not that I can tell. As long as we don't detach and no one looks too closely at the *Goliath*'s hull, we should be fine. It's not magic, though."

Jax slipped his boots on, grabbing a vest and throwing it on as he exited his quarters.

Skip continued, "Looks like we're in the Anchorage system."

"Anchorage? There's nothing in Anchorage," Jax said. He stopped at the kitchen and grabbed a bottle of water. The Anchorage system was at least considerably closer than Tycho station.

Dropping into his seat on the bridge, he said, "I stand corrected." Outside the transparent hull was a space station. Nothing like Kelso, but a station all the same. It was about a fifth the size of Kelso and looked like a four-leaf clover, if the leaves were thick triangles. Arrayed around the small station were the ships of the Nemesis Fleet that had been taken. Several had already docked with the petals of the station. The *Goliath* was sliding into place in the center of the loose formation of captured derelicts.

"What're we looking at?" Jax asked.

Rudy chimed in first. "It's a Mark Two Regula StarLabs model station. They didn't ship with much in the way of weapons beyond a few anti-piracy blaster turrets. Probably why it's out here, out of the way."

"Without main sensors, there is no way to tell how many people are aboard," Skip added. "From the marketing brochure for that model, I would say no more than a hundred. Maybe two, though I would guess most of this crew shipped out on that carrier."

Rudy added, "They are broadcasting an ident, so whatever this all is, it's at least quasi-legal."

Jax ran a hand over his face. When he realized the pair was done talking, he said, "Sorry, I tuned you two out. Weapons?"

There was a judgmental moment of silence before Skip answered, "As I mentioned, the station does not have many weapons, and none are much of a threat to us. However, all of the Nemesis ships are armed. From what we saw back at the staging area, they're crewed by the bare minimum needed to get them underway. I doubt they can power up their guns right now."

"Then here we go," Jax said. He reached over to the landing gear control. "I still can't believe this worked."

Rudy beeped. "It wouldn't have if the *Goliath* was at full power and had working sensors."

With a clunk and a groan, the magnetics in the landing gear disengaged. The *Osprey* drifted away from the massive dreadnaught.

"Blah, blah," Jax said. He pressed another control, retracting the gear. "Let's do this." He powered up the reactor, rewarded immediately by the thrusters kicking in. "Skip..."

"Already transmitting. Tight beam," the ship's SI replied.

Aboard the *Goliath*, Lieutenant Ardoin screamed, "What is it with that pissant? Can't he see he that he lost? The fleet is mine!" He spun to the woman he had been working with since recalling all of Piotr Fuller's remaining salvagers. They were in the CIC, having spent the last two days working on restoring function to the massive ship.

Once they got the service droids back online, things progressed rapidly. Entire sections of the ship were back online. The reactor was operating at fifty percent, more than enough for navigation and weapons.

Beatrice, the ranking salvager, turned to look at the annoying Imperial, her brown eyes glinting in the overhead lighting. "He seems as motivated as you. Kindred spirits?"

"Rank amateur," Ardoin hissed. On one of the large displays set around the perimeter, the Valerian Coop Infiltrator was zipping in between the ships of the Nemesis Fleet and the station ahead.

"Doesn't look very amateur," the woman mumbled under her breath. She turned to the console nearest her, bringing up the communication system. "Home base, this is Beatrice Abumwe. Fuller is dead. The *Lucky Lady* is lost. We're still on the job, I'm in command."

"Who's the asshole in the infiltrator?" the operator aboard the space station asked. On one of the displays nearby the station's limited weapons were tracking and firing on the small attacker.

"Competition," Beatrice replied. "Scramble teams to the ships. We've got to get them moving."

"Look!" someone shouted. On a large display, the smaller ship was disgorging missiles, lots of them. By the look of it, every missile that the small ship had left.

"What the ...?" Ardoin said. On the screen, missiles streaked this way and that, none heading for the defenseless station. "He's attacking the derelicts?"

"Crippling them," Beatrice added.

On the display, missiles streaked in to explode against the engines of the old ships, ensuring that they wouldn't be going anywhere anytime soon.

The small ship lobbed another salvo of missiles, then vanished into a wormhole. The ships of the Nemesis Fleet were drifting randomly, engines nothing more than sparking ruins. None of them were going anywhere any time soon.

When the wormhole opened, and the *Osprey* returned to normal space, the Nemesis Fleet was just like when Jax and Rudy left four days ago, except there were three other ships mixed in. The new arrivals were considerably more modern.

"We are being hailed," Skip announced.

On the small comm screen, a face appeared, a familiar one. It wasn't Naomi. "You can't seem to stay out trouble, can you?"

Jax huffed. "Hi. Naomi got through, I see."

The other man nodded. "She did. We just got here an hour or so ago, actually. This place is pretty off the beaten path." He gestured to something beyond the camera pickup.

"Yeah, explains why no one found it until now," Jax said. The other man nodded. He added, "It's a good thing I'm just that—"

The commander cut him off. "Naomi already filled me in."

"Traitor," Jax whispered, looking down at his console to adjust course for what looked like the command ship for the three new arrivals. He smiled. "Well, anyway."

"Come aboard, I'll fill you in." The commander smiled and closed the comm.

The *Spirit of Independence* was big. Old, but not Nemesis Fleet old. Jax did not know where the commander had found the old relic, or the two light cruisers flanking it. He also did not particularly care.

The largest of the three ships was maybe half as big as one of the Empire's heavies. Impressive, but no match for the Empire, which was why Jax still wanted nothing to do with what he considered a lost cause.

"Hey, Partner," Naomi greeted from the opposite end of the conference room table, when Jax and Rudy entered. Rudy rolled over to stand next to Baxter. Next to Naomi sat the commander and one of his subordinates.

The commander gestured for Jax to sit. "I know you don't want to be involved with us, but—"

"Still don't." Jax held up a hand and looked at Naomi. "You did tell him I wanted a reward, right?"

Naomi stared at him, eyes flat. "I'm not new."

"That's it? Money? That's all you two care about?" The commander leaned forward.

"Yup."

"More or less." Naomi inclined her head.

The commander stood. "Fair enough." He turned to his subordinate. "Mara, get them paid." He started for the door, then stopped. "You know, we might actually stand a chance in all this, if more people like you got involved." He didn't wait for a reply, letting the hatch slide closed behind him.

On a display mounted to the bulkhead, Jax and Naomi watched as tugs flitted about between the remaining ships.

Each tug was little more than a powerful wormhole generator mounted to equally powerful thrusters with a small crew cabin bolted on. Each tug was attached to a ship by thick cables magnetically attached to hard points along the larger vessel's hulls.

Mara, whom Jax recognized from his visit to the Rebellion's headquarters on New Terra, smiled. "I'll be back in a few minutes."

Jax nodded absently, his eyes still on the display and the careful dance the tugs were doing with the much larger antique warships.

Jax's gPhone beeped, causing him and Naomi to jump.

"You have a signal?" Naomi asked.

Jax shrugged, reaching for his gPhone. "This thing must have a pretty powerful comm node." He gestured to the ship around them. He looked at the screen, a groan escaping his lips.

Naomi leaned in to look at the screen. "Might as well get this over with while you're a safe distance." She grinned.

Jax sighed and swiped on the phone. The large display he and Naomi were standing in front of switched from the external camera view to the larger-than-life, scowling faces of Marshall and Steve Delphino.

"You fucking asshole!" the older, bigger Delphino shouted. "We've been calling you for a week!"

Steve leaned in. "Where are you? Did you find the fleet? You know you owe us?"

Marshall shouldered his brother back. "Owe us big time. That grungy nobody Abano and his group were ready to put a plasma round in our brain pans when you left LV-426."

Steve tried to get back into the frame, his mouth open to lob another demand or insult. Jax held up both hands. "You're right, guys. We're sorry."

"We?" Naomi said. She leaned away from Jax and looked at the screen. "I wasn't included in this decision."

"Traitor," Jax whispered under his breath. He said, louder, "We shoulda kept you both in the loop. We...I...got greedy."

"Blah blah, Caruso. I'm gonna beat your ass until you can't eat solid foods," Marshall growled.

"We'll cut you in," Jax said.

That seemed to mollify both Delphinos.

"How much?" Steve demanded.

"Forty percent," Jax said. Before either Delphino could reply, he added, "Things went sideways out here. Half the fleet was lost. Long story."

"We figured. It's been all over INS for a few days," Steve said, considerably calmer.

Naomi looked at Jax, then the two men on screen. "What's been all over INS?"

Marshall's face scrunched up. "Hold on." The view changed as he did something on his gPhone. Jax and Naomi both looked away as the view shifted and tilted wildly.

"Tap that," Steve said. "No, that. Yeah. Now, no, no. Listen."

"Fuck you, Stevie," Marshall growled.

Finally, the image on the display returned to the two large faces. "Here," Marshall said. An icon appeared indicating that another data stream was coming. On his gPhone, Jax tapped *accept*.

A window appeared over Steve's face. The Imperial News Service logo was frozen mid rotation.

Before Jax or Naomi could say anything, the INS logo resumed its rotation, then vanished, to be replaced by a stylish news anchor in a bespoke suit. "Earlier today, intelligence officials announced that a months' long operation investigating illegal salvage came to a head with several arrests and a minor skirmish in the Anchorage system." The blonde-haired anchor turned to a new camera. "The apparent ringleader of the operation was an Imperial naval officer out of Tycho station. It seems this officer, along with several others, was running an illegal salvage scam, wherein the Empire hired a legit salvage company only for that company to turn around and sell on the black market the salvage they'd been paid to destroy or recycle."

Jax leaned back and looked at Naomi, fist held up for bumping. She looked at him, then back to the Delphinos. She grinned and offered her fist. "I love it when a plan comes together." Jax grinned.

The video window closed. "You can't ever do anything simple, huh?"

"Where would be the fun in that?" Jax asked.

The hatch opened and Mara walked in. Jax looked at her, then back to the Delphino brothers.

A moment before Jax closed the call, Steve said, "Forty percent."

The wall display went black, then returned to showing the salvage operation going on outside.

Mara went over the payment details, explaining that due to the nature of the Rebellion's financing, the payment would come from no fewer than eight sources, but the sum would be the agreed upon amount.

When the junior officer left the conference room, Naomi turned to Jax. "Forty percent?"

"Seemed fair." Jax shrugged.

"To who?"

"Whom," Rudy corrected, then wheeled back quickly to avoid Naomi's angry swipe.

"We have to live on the same station as them. They're, sort of, our friends."

"Your friends," she corrected.

He shrugged. "I really was a jerk. Steve was there when we overheard Abano. Cutting them out, especially when they coulda been killed, was a shitty thing to do."

Naomi nodded. "No argument."

"To which part?" Jax asked.

"All of it," Naomi said. She turned toward the door.

"But I'm handsome," Jax said, then added, "Right?"

From the corridor, Naomi shouted, "Sure, whatever. Come on, dreamboat. Let's get the hell out of here. No telling how long the lanky creep lasted under interrogation. The Empire's gotta be on its way."

He turned to the two droids still in the room with him. "I think I liked it better when it was just us."

"You'd have a lot more black eyes if that were still the case," Baxter said, stomping out of the room.

The End.

If you enjoyed this story, I'd love it if you left a review.
Seriously, reviews are a big deal.

Reviews help readers find authors. Reviews help books get
discovered.
Even just "I liked it" means a lot!

Want to stay up to date on the happenings in the Grand Human Empire?
Sign up for my newsletter at
johnwilker.com/newsletter
Visit me online at
johnwilker.com

If you like supporting things you love by sporting merch or buying direct, well you're in luck! I've launched a shop, take a look. **Use, discount code "Osprey" and you'll save %15!**

As they say, there's no harm in asking, so here we go.

If you can help connect me with someone who can get The Grand human Empire on a screen (Big or Little) I'll cut you in for 10% (Up to $10,000) of whatever advance is paid.

Send me an email and we can discuss.
rights@johnwilker.com

John Wilker lives in Denver Colorado with his wife Nicole. He loves telling stories about the future.

9 781951 964085